His Trust

His Guardians Book 6

by

Ronna Bacon

Proverbs 3:5-6
Trust in the Lord with all your heart and lean
not unto your own understanding.
In all your ways acknowledge Him and He
shall direct your path.

Table of Contents

Prologue

She watched quietly from a corner as the money changed hands and crates were quickly unloaded into the storage area of the shop. What was that, she wondered? At this time of day, who would be bringing in stock? It was dark and wet. She clasped her hand over her mouth to keep from crying out as she recognized one man and then the youth with him. What were they mixed up in?

She crept as silently as she could from the corner she had been hiding from, throwing glances over her shoulder, praying no one saw her. An accidental kick to a discarded pop tin brought voices behind her and she shrunk back into the darkness, relieved when she heard them say it's just a cat. She didn't move for the longest time, waiting and counting the different footsteps she heard. Finally, she took a quick peek behind her and then moved out again on silent feet. Once she felt safe, she began to run. No one would believe her, she thought. Who would believe a mere child over the word of a trusted store owner?

She crept into her home and up to her room, silently slipping under the covers.

Lord, she prayed, let no one know what I saw,
that I was there. I'm so afraid.

Chapter 1

The sun was just peeking over the horizon and the birds starting their early morning chorus as Abigail Gilmore stepped out onto her back deck. She loved this time of the morning. She drew in a deep breath of the air scented with the flowers and the faint odour of fresh-cut grass. Her dogs romped through the fenced yard in the early morning dew as her gray tabby wound around her legs. Sipping her tea, she drew a deep breath. She had some work she needed to finish today, then she was taking a break for a few days. Working as a court transcriptionist was interesting work, but it was tedious and at times wearing on her soul. She shook her head to clear it of her thoughts and then walked back into her home. She needed to get on the way but she hesitated. What is it about day, Lord, she asked? Why do I have such a feeling of trouble and pain and worry weighing me down this morning?

Climbing up the stairs to the courthouse later that morning, Abigail nodded and smiled at the workers she knew. She headed for the court reporter's office. It was a busy place that morning, she thought, scanning the people sitting and standing around. She headed for the gate to the counter and went through, hearing complaints about that behind her. Mary, the clerk, smiled and nodded at her, then turned to the people complaining.

"She works for us, so be quiet, or you'll be at the back of the line."

Abigail shook her head at that. Mary knew how to keep her people in control. She stopped, feeling a sense of foreboding as she turned in a circle. Where was it and who was it?

Mid-afternoon, Abigail rose from her desk and stretched. The trial she was transcribing was finished and saved to the system. She was glad. It had been a long trial over many weeks. She snuck a peek at her watch. No, her cousin, Judge Jordan Gilmore, would still be in his afternoon trial session, so she couldn't arrange to meet him for a late lunch.

As she opened the door to the office she had been working in, shouts and then cries from the front office area startled her. She heard popping sounds and wondered what that was. She drew in a deep breath, fear coursing through her as she heard the gruff voices of men heading her way.

"She has to be here somewhere. We need her."

"There aren't many places to hide." A second voice was even coarser.

Abigail looked around. She wouldn't have time to make it to the back door. Where, she thought? Lord, help me, I need a hiding place right now.

She turned, hand still on the closed office door. Locking it would only give them a clue that she was here. She ducked back from the door, desperate to find that hiding spot.

Luke Cavanagh, one of Rebel's Elite Security team, sat in the back row of the courtroom. He and Nathaniel Graeme, a fellow team member, had been called to give expert evidence that morning in an ongoing trial and had been asked to stay for the rest of the day, just in case they were needed for cross-examination. The judge looked up as a bailiff slipped in and spoke quietly to the two men, who stood and followed him out. Judge Jordan Gilmore's attention stayed on the door for a minute, then returned to the lawyers arguing in front of him. If there was a need for him to know, the bailiff would have approached him.

Luke and Nathaniel headed towards Frankie Brennan, a friend and detective on the local force, standing near a staircase, eyes constantly on the move.

"Frankie, what's going on?"

Frankie spun, a harried look on his face, that smoothed out as he saw the two. "Luke, Nathaniel. I'm glad you two are here. Doug and the ETF teams are tied up out front with a shooter. We have to clear the offices along the second floor. We've had an active shooting in the court reporter's office. There is still a clerk in one of the offices that we can't get to from the front, but there's a back door. I don't have anyone available and trained in hostage situations who can get in and get her and then get back out."

"Get us our weapons, Frankie." Luke looked surprised as Frankie handed them over. "You were ready."

"That I was." He spoke as he led the way to stairs at the other end of the hallway. "If we go up to the second floor and then head to the right, it will take us to a corridor that leads to the back door of the office. Here's the key to it."

Nathaniel looked down as he took the key. "How many men and what weapons?"

"Word is two and hand guns. We've been told we have casualties in the reception area. How many, I don't know yet. There should only be the one woman in a back office. From what I'm told, it's the second office on your right when you go in."

Luke and Nathaniel exchanged glances as they headed with soft steps towards the door. This was not unusual for them, to head in to rescue a hostage, but they were short the other six on their team.

Luke's hand went up with three fingers raised. Nathaniel nodded. As the end of the count down, he tried the door, surprised that it was unlocked. Carefully opening it, they crept in, senses alert for anyone who would come at them. The door to the office they wanted was closed. Luke's hand on the knob, they waited and listened. Opening the door, he looked around, a puzzled look on his face. Nathaniel's face mirrored his. Luke quietly shut the door as they peered around the office. Nathaniel's hand on his arm brought Luke's attention around and to the small space between the office wall and the filing cabinet. The woman had tucked herself down in there, head on her knees.

On silent feet, Luke moved towards her, then crouched down beside her.

"Ma'am?" When she didn't respond, he shot a look at Nathaniel, then tried again. "Ma'am?" He reached out a hand and touched her arm, causing her to jump and her own hand to go to her mouth.

Luke stilled as he recognized an old friend. Abi? What was she doing here?

"Abi?" She didn't respond to his voice. He reached and drew her to her feet. "Come on, Abi GG, we need to get you out of here."

Nathaniel shot him a look when he said the name, then moved back to crack open the door as Luke gathered Abigail up in his arms.

"My purse. If you leave my purse, they'll find me."

Nathaniel grabbed her purse from the floor where she had dropped it and handed it to her before heading out the door, motioning for Luke to follow. Silent steps took them out the door and down the stairs to the outside. Walking as far away from the building as he could, Luke finally set Abigail on her feet, keeping an arm around her to steady her.

"Abi, are you hurt?" He patiently waited as focus returned to her eyes.

"Luke? What? Where did you come from?" Then terror took over and she clutched at his arms. "Don't let them find me, please."

"Who, Abi? Don't let who find you?" Luke's eyes on her face, he studied the fear, no terror, he thought, that filled it.

Nathaniel turned. "We need to get her right away from here, Luke. I let Frankie know we have her and we're heading for Rebel's. She's not injured, is she?"

"Abi, are you hurt?" Again, Luke waited until she shook her head.

"No, I'm not. I need to see Jordan." She struggled to break free from him, but he just tightened his arms until she became still.

"Jordan?"

"My cousin. He's a judge here."

Luke finally made the connection between the judge and Abi. "We'll get word to him, Abi. Just let us get you out of here." Luke's voice was soothing.

Nathaniel nodded, his phone already out to send a text to Frankie. "Let's move, Luke. Who knows if there is someone else around involved."

Luke tucked her into the back of his truck, then headed for Rebel's, eyes constantly on the move.

Nathaniel shot a look back at Abigail, sitting still, eyes closed, a look of fear on her face still. "How do you know her, Luke?"

"Abi GG? We grew up together. She was my best friend." He threw a quick look back at her. "I didn't know she was here in town. Her cousin is the judge whose courtroom we were in today. I knew he was here."

"Where'd she get that nickname?"

A voice from the back spoke up in a disgruntled manner. "That's his version of my name. You'll never give it up, will you, Lukie?"

Nathaniel broke out in laugher, as Luke smiled. "That I won't, Abigail Grace Gilmore."

"Where are we going? It doesn't look like the road to my home."

"We're taking you out to Rebel's. Frankie Brennan, a detective on the scene today, asked us to."

Abigail shrugged, already thinking of what she needed to get done that day. "I need

to go home, Luke. I have dogs and a cat to
take care of."

Chapter 2

Abe Finlay, team leader to Rebel's Elite Security, walked towards Nathaniel as he headed away from Luke's truck, then stopped as Luke helped a young woman from the back of his truck. His eyes narrowing, he moved towards Nathaniel.

"Nathaniel, talk to me. I thought you were testifying today, not gathering up strays."

Nathaniel shot a glance over at Luke and Abigail, then back at Abe. "She's not a stray, Abe. There was an incident in the courthouse today, and Frankie pulled us out of the courtroom to help in a hostage situation. Abigail Gilmore here is who we rescued. Apparently she's an old friend of Luke's."

Abe turned as Luke and Abigail stopped near him. "Welcome, Abigail, to Rebel's. How about Luke takes you into the house?"

She shook her head. "I need to go home. I have dogs and a cat to look after. I can't be away from home."

Abe shot a look at Luke, who shook his head. "I tried to tell her we'd go get them, but she's not hearing me."

Abe nodded. "Take her on up to the house, Luke, and if you can get her address and her keys, we'll get her animals for her." As they walked away, Abe watched, then spoke. "What's the real story, Nathaniel?"

He shrugged. "We don't know it all, Abe, other than she's a court reporter and there was a hostage incident there. I'm not sure what all happened, Frankie didn't say. He did say he'd be out this evening and asked if we could keep Abigail under guard until then."

Abe nodded, then headed for the house, Nathaniel at his side. "Is Jordan Gilmore related to her?"

"A cousin, I think Luke said. You don't think it's related to him, do you?"

"Too early yet to speculate, Nathaniel. It might be." He looked around. "When we get her keys, take Joseph with you and go get her animals. We'll keep them here for today and then see."

Early evening, Frankie stood at Abe's door, sorrow in his heart. It had not been a good day, he thought, lives lost and others changed. What could Abigail Gilmore tell him? He didn't know her but had an acquaintance with her cousin. He had yet to speak in depth with Jordan.

Abe watched his long-time friend and saw the effects of the day on him. It wasn't often Frankie showed his emotions, having been an undercover street cop before making detective.

"Frankie, come on in. What's happened?"

Frankie stepped in onto the dark hardwood floor of the hallway. He stared at Abe for a minute, then sighed. "It's been a bad day, Abe. We have four people dead, another six injured. Mary, our clerk in the office, is one of the dead. We talked to the injured. Whoever these men were, they were after Abigail and knew she would be there today. How did they not find her?"

Abe shrugged, then pointed towards his office. "Luke said she had burrowed into a small space beside a filing cabinet that was hid when the door opened. She hasn't said anything, other than wanting her dogs and cat."

Frankie shot him a look. "Her animals?"

Abe nodded. "I spoke with her cousin, Jordan. He was going to go get them and take them to his mother's. I made sure he had someone with him when he went."

"Thanks, Abe." Frankie stopped at the doorway to the office, studying Abigail where she sat on the couch. "She looks fragile, Abe. I'm not sure how much information I'll get from her."

Abe stopped him with a hand on his arm. "Just so you know, Luke and she are old friends. Nathaniel told me Luke said she was his best friend when they were growing up. She's been really quiet. Luke indicated that's not her."

Frankie nodded, lost in thought. That just put a whole new aspect to this, Lord. I see Your hand in this. Maybe Luke can get her to talk.

"Abigail?" Frankie stopped in from her, watching intently as she jumped and then looked up. "I'm Frankie Brennan, detective with the Riverville force. I need to ask you some questions."

Abigail began shaking her head. "No. I don't know anything. I didn't see them."

Frankie sank down into a chair across from her. "That's okay, Abigail. I just need to know what you heard, if you heard anything."

She shook her head. "I can't. I'm sorry."

Frankie looked up at Abe, then at Luke, who nodded and slid down beside Abigail, his hand reaching for hers.

"Abi, talk to me. Tell me what happened."

Her brown eyes huge and troubled, she stared at Luke. "I didn't see anything, Luke. Nothing. I had finished the transcripts of the trial and was getting ready to leave. I remember checking my watch, thinking I could get Jordan to go for lunch, then heard some commotion from the front. A popping sound. Some yells, some cries. Then I heard two men." She stopped, her body shaking with fear. "They were looking for me, Luke. What did they want?"

"Did they say anything?" Luke pushed, knowing just how far he could.

She shook her head again. "Just that they knew I was there and in one of the offices. I didn't lock the door, thinking they would know that's where I was. I prayed they didn't find me and that I could find some place to hide."

Luke reached to wrap an arm around his old friend. "You did good, Abi GG. You did good." He looked up at Frankie, who nodded for him to continue. "What about the voices? Did you recognize them?"

She stared across the room, then spoke. "No, I've never heard them before. They didn't have any accents, both gruff and coarse. One sounded like he was a heavy smoker, he had that tone to the voice." She looked over at Frankie. "I'm sorry. I can't tell you much."

Frankie tucked his notebook back into his pocket. "You've done fine, Abigail. No one else saw them leave. They've had to have gone by your office and out the back door. It should have been locked and wasn't. If you think of anything else, Abe here can get in touch with me." He stood, staring down at her, the soft lamp light playing off her auburn hair. "I want you to stay here with Abe for now, just until we can get things figured out a bit better." At her protest, he continued, "We don't know who they are. If they know you worked at the courthouse, chances are they know where you live. And before you ask, Abe says Jordan had gone to get your animals and taken them to your aunt's."

Abigail stared up at Frankie, horror on her face. "What about Aunt Mel and Jordan?"

"Jordan has protection with federal officers. He's making sure your aunt is guarded. Abe here will take care of you. Right now, we don't have a lot to go on, it's too early in the investigation."

Abigail looked down, then back up at Frankie. "Tell me. How many were hurt?"

A look of distress flickered across Frankie's face, then he spoke. "I'm sorry, Abigail. We have four fatalities and six wounded."

"Mary?" Her question was quiet, then she buried her head against Luke as she saw the sorrow on Frankie's face.

"Mary didn't make it, Abigail. I'm sorry for your loss."

"They're dead because of me?" Her question was muffled against Luke's shirt.

"We don't know that for sure, Abigail." Frankie hesitated as he watched the sobs shake her body, then he turned, beckoning to Abe to follow him.

"Can you keep her safe, Abe? We're pretty sure she was the target today."

"As always, we'll do our best. She'll have a load to work through, coming to grips with that." Abe shot a look behind him into the office, to the two sitting on the couch. "Having Luke here will help, I hope."

"It might. I pray it does. Our town's hurting, Abe, and we need to bring this to a close quickly."

"Let me know if there's anything we can do."

Abe hesitated before he headed back to the office, heading down the hall to the room Abigail would be staying in. He dropped the bag Jordan had packed and Frankie had brought out for her on the floor near the desk, then turned to the bed, reaching for the bedside light. He stopped, his mind drifting through what Abigail had said and then on to how they could keep her safe against an unknown enemy. It wasn't the first time for this, but each time, he hoped it would be the last.

Please, Lord, help us to keep her safe. Another lady needs our protection and I don't know how much more my guys can take of this.

Chapter 3

Standing staring out the patio door the next morning, Abe sipped at his cup of coffee, pondering the news from the day before. I don't understand, Lord, why or who but You do. You've placed Abigail into our care. Help us to keep her safe. He heard a whisper of sock-covered feet on the floor and saw Luke's reflection in the glass.

"Is Abigail still sleeping, Luke?"

Luke shook his head. "I haven't heard anything from her room. I thought I'd check in a few minutes." He stood, staring out the kitchen window before shaking his head and reaching for a mug and the coffee carafe. "I didn't even know she was in town, Abe. The last time I talked to Mom, she didn't say anything. Abigail has had a habit of moving around every little while, sometimes only staying a few months in a place before moving on."

"Restless or wanderlust?" Abe's question caught Luke off guard.

"I'm not sure, Abe. This isn't what she was like when we were growing up." Luke turned to lean against the counter, his eyes on the doorway to the hall. "She stayed very close to home and family."

"What happened when you went to college?"

Luke thought about that, then shrugged, finally running his hand through his dark brown close cropped curls. His green eyes sought out Abe's face. "Nothing that I ever heard about. She went to a different college than I did. We didn't see each other much when we were in school, and then afterwards, the odd phone call, the odd letter. It's like she was hiding something."

Abe nodded. "We need to find out why she cut communications with you, Luke, to see if it has any bearing on what happened yesterday."

Luke's eyes shot to Abe again, then back to the hallway. "We can try, Abe, but something I don't think it will work. She can be very close mouthed when she decides to be. I'm worried about her though. Yesterday is going to be a rough one for her to work through."

"It will be. Maybe if she talks with Greg Evans, the pastor, or with Doug's

Darcy, it might help." Abe turned as he heard footsteps in the hall. "Sounds like your friend is up. I'll let you break the news to her that she's stuck with us for the duration."

Luke nodded, knowing in his heart she would fight him and them, unless she had changed a lot in the last ten years or so. He watched as Abigail hesitated in the doorway, the uncertainty not her.

"Good morning, Abi. How did you sleep?"

Abigail looked up at her friend and thought, when did he get so tall? I don't remember that height. "All right, I guess. It was restless, but I did get some sleep." The black circles under her eyes belied that.

"What can I get you to drink or eat?" Luke pulled a chair out for her, then hand on her arm, made her sit. Concern in his eyes, he watched as she complied. Something's off, Lord, and I don't know what.

"Just some tea, if there's any tea." She looked around the large kitchen, taking it in. "Is this Abe's house?"

"It is, Abi." Luke studied her, knowing that she had been told that the night before. "Talk to me, Abi." He set the tea in front of her, then sat where he could watch her face.

She shook her head. "I need to leave, Luke. I need to leave here and leave this town."

"That's not happening, Abi. Right now, you're a witness to murder and Caleb Logan, our police chief, has put you under our protection." Her eyes shot up to him, a puzzled look on her face. Luke sighed, knowing he had to explain further. "Abe runs a security company. While we do mostly training now, there are times we're called into provide protection and security for people. Right now, that's you." He hesitated, then continued, "If you're not under our protection, then Caleb is going to stick you away in a safe house somewhere and you'll have no contact with any of your family. With us, you'll have a certain amount of freedom."

She looked at him, then down at the mug she was rubbing with her thumb. She sighed, knowing he was right. "I don't like this, Luke."

"I know you don't." He looked down at his own mug. "What happened, Abi? What happened to chase you away from your family? Your Mom says you hardly ever come home anymore, and that's not you."

She stilled and he saw a shadow cross her face. Then, she looked up at him, and he saw the fear in her eyes. "I saw something years ago, Luke, that I shouldn't have seen. I've been running ever since."

"Why didn't you talk to me?"

She shook her head. "I couldn't. I mean, I wanted to, but I was so afraid that he would come after all my family and friends."

"Who?" Luke looked up to see Matt and Joseph standing in the doorway, listening quietly.

She sat back, her eyes searching the distance past. She then shook her head again. "I don't know who he is, but he follows me every place I go. I haven't seen him in a couple of years and I thought I was safe here. After yesterday, I wonder if I am."

"What did you see, Abi?"

"I saw him kill someone." Her voice broke as tears gathered in her eyes. "He must have heard me and chased after me. I hid and got away, but somehow he seems to have gotten my name. He's followed me for years."

Luke's heart sank as he realized the fear she had been living with. "Do you know who was killed?"

She shook her head. "I don't, but if I give Frankie the town and the date, can he find out and maybe stop this?"

At this point, Joseph had left to go find Abe. He needed to hear what Abigail was saying.

Luke nodded. "Let me have the information. We'll get it to Frankie for you."

Frankie looked up from his paperwork at the knock at his door, then beckoned Abe in. "What brings you in, Abe?"

Abe sat, his eyes on his folded hands, then looked up. "Luke talked to Abigail this morning. We're not sure if what she said has any bearing on what happened yesterday or not." He pulled a slip of paper from his shirt pocket and studied it for a moment before handing it over to Frankie. "She gave us this town and date. Apparently, she witnessed a murder years ago and has been on the run ever since."

Frankie's hand stilled as he reached for the paper. "Seriously? What is it with all these ladies your guys get involved with?"

Abe gave a half-smile, then shrugged. "I have no idea, Frankie, but it seems God has bigger plans than we do."

Frankie opened the slip of paper and read, his body going still as he did so. "Do you know what this is, Abe?"

Abe shook his head, eyes on his friend. "I take it you do, though."

Frankie nodded. "Luke's friend is involved in something really deep here, Abe. And she's been on the run?"

Abe nodded. "From what Luke said, she has been and whoever it is has been following her. What is it?"

"If my memory is correct, I can remember this coming through the wires when I was just getting started on the force. A banker was murdered, and it came out that he had been laundering money for a crime family. I can't remember what all they were involved in right at the moment, but they had a far-reaching crime empire. The authorities have been trying to bring them down for years, nibbling away at the lower echelons, but not getting to the top ones." He looked up at Abe. "I'm afraid Luke's friend is involved in this. That would explain yesterday."

Abe nodded as he stood. "Luke has told her she has to stay with us, or Caleb would lock her away somewhere."

"It's better if she stays with you, Abe. That way, we have a better chance of keeping her alive. Who knows who they've reached on any of the forces."

Chapter 4

Abigail turned as she heard footsteps on the wooden floor of the living room approaching her. Abe stopped just short of where she had been standing, looking out the front window. She looks lost, he thought, lost, alone and afraid.

"Abigail, come sit for a minute." Abe motioned to one of the chairs behind her and watched as she sank on the edge, apprehension in her demeanour.

"What do you know?" Her eyes never left his face.

Abe sighed to himself as he sat. This was not going to be easy, after all, is it, Lord? You give me the difficult ones to deal with. Speak through me, please.

"I spoke with Frankie and he recognized the city and date without having to do any research on it." He hesitated, not quite sure how to proceed.

"It's always best just to say it out loud. At least, that's what my Mom tells me."

He searched her face and then nodded. She looked fragile and dainty, but there was an underlying strength there that most people would overlook on a superficial glance at her.

"The date and place? There was a banker murdered by a hired assassin, hired by a mob family. We can't be sure if that's who is still after you or not. Frankie would like you to come in and take a look at some pictures."

She nodded as her eyes moved past Abe to Luke standing in the hall doorway. "I can do that. I need to end this, Abe. I am tired of looking over my shoulder, of waiting for a phone call that says one of my family members or friends have been killed because of me." She stopped to draw in a deep breath, tears in her eyes. "Just like Mary and those others. Will their families blame me?"

Abe shook his head. "We don't know if this is who it was or not. We're not sure why those two men were after you. Caleb's PR team is working on a statement to release tomorrow. It will simply state that it is unknown who the gunmen were after." He stopped as a thought crossed his mind, and he looked over as Luke came and sat in a chair near Abigail. "Who else usually works in that office or in an office near that one?"

She sat back, eyes never leaving his face. "Are you suggesting that I wasn't the target after all, that another transcriptionist might have been?" At his nod, her eyes closed as she thought, then she spoke, giving him names.

"I'll get these to Frankie. In the meanwhile, what can we do to make it easier for you?"

"If I had my computer, I could still work." As he shook his head, she frowned. "What? You don't want me working?"

"That's not it, Abi." Luke spoke up and her frown was directed at him. He smiled at her, then spoke again. "Have you noticed anything off about your place?"

She thought, then nodded. "A few weeks ago, it felt like someone had been in the house, but I have a good security system and thought I had just forgotten where I had put some documents. They were moved from where I thought I had left them."

Abe stood. "Let me have the name of your security company, Abigail. I'll have Joseph contact them, or if we can have your keys, he'll go take a look at your panel as well. It may well be that you're right and someone has been in your home. As to work, if you can bring up your transcription system on any computer, I have an extra one in the office you can use. It has very high security on it and no one would be able to track where you are."

Abigail looked at him in astonishment. Other than her family, over the past few years, she had not met anyone as kind as he and his men were. She knew from Luke that five of the men were now engaged. She nodded and rose. "Let me get them for you." She stopped and turned. "Abe, can you ask him to bring me something? There is a locked box in my closet, on the floor behind the shoes. If Joseph could bring that and the Bible by my bed, I'd like that."

"Anything else?"

She shook her head. "No. Jordan did well last night with what he packed for me. He knows me well. Jeans and T-shirts and my fancy socks are all I need."

Luke waited until he heard her go into the bedroom, then turned to Abe. In a quiet voice, he asked, "How safe is she really, Abe?"

Abe shrugged. "Frankie's looking into that connection as well as anything else he can thing of. They're investigating everyone who was in the office yesterday and those who should have been and weren't. The federal office is looking into Jordan to see if there's a connection there. Frankie was passing on the information Abigail gave you." He turned to look towards the hall. "How's she doing?"

Luke shook his head. "She's hiding. When she gets scared or hurt, she hides. She always has. Not even her parents or her siblings could see it. I always did."

"You have a connection with her that they don't. Use it if you have to, Luke, to keep her safe." He stood as he heard Abigail coming back and took the keys from her as well as the slip of paper with her pass code on it. "I'll have Joseph change this, just in case."

"Thank you, Abe." She moved past him to sit once again, lost in thought. The men's eyes met, then Abe moved away.

Abigail sat in silence for a while, then turned to Luke. "What is it, Luke? What is it you're not telling me?"

He shrugged. "There's nothing to tell, Abi. Abe told you what we know or don't know." He watched the conflicting emotions crossing her face. "Do you want to call your Mom?"

Her eyes flew to him, she started to nod, then shook her head. "It would be too easy for them to trace a call. I think that's how they've found me in the past."

Luke nodded. "More than likely." He pulled out his phone and handed it to her. "This one can't be traced. Go on, call her." He stood and studied his friend, seeing the changes the years had worked in her beautiful face. "I'll be in the back yard. Come find me when you're done." He was gone before she could even frame a thank you.

Luke turned his head as Abigail approached across the deck to where he was sitting on the steps and handed him his phone. He pocketed it and then pulled her down beside him, wrapping her in a hug. She swiped at the tears on her face.

"Did you get to talk to your Mom?"

She nodded, unable to speak for a moment. "I told her what was happening and that they needed to take care. She was so upset, Lukie. She wanted me to come home right away." She swiped at her face once again as the tears continued. "I told her I couldn't take a chance. Thank you for letting me use your phone."

"You can use it to call your Mom any time you want to." Luke tightened his hold on her. "Now what, Abi GG?"

She shrugged, her head coming down on his shoulder. "I don't know, Luke. I just want this over. I feel like I've had my life on hold for ten years and I'm ready to move on."

"I know you are. God has you here at this point for a reason, Abi. This may be why. Frankie and Abe's uncle, Eddie, will investigate it thoroughly. They're really good at this. Caleb will work with them. If we have to, we'll bring in Abe's brother-in-law, Gideon, a private investigator. We also know someone who can track people like no other." He turned his head slightly as he heard a noise behind him and saw Abe standing, watching, compassion on his face. "Even more than that, each of the guys here will protect you, with their lives if necessary."

She shook her head. "No, Luke. I can't ask that."

"You didn't. We were asked and we agreed. It's what we do best, Abi, keeping people safe. Just so you know, Matt, Nathaniel, Micah, Ian and Joseph have been through this with their ladies."

She turned to look at him. "Their ladies? But I'm not your lady, Luke."

No, he thought, not yet, but Lord willing, you will be. He repeated his words.

"We've been asked and agreed to it. You're my friend, Abi. That's all that matters to them. If they can do that for strangers, they'll be more than willing to help keep a friend safe. Besides, they weren't the guys' ladies until it was all over."

She shook her head, then just sat, thinking of what had gone on. *Lord, I want this over. What will it take?*

Joseph turned from his computer monitor as Abe entered the office, deep in thought.

"Is she okay, Abe?"

Abe looked up, bringing his thoughts back to the present. "She is. Luke had her call her parents. I'm not sure how that went, but Luke seems to have it under control."

Joseph nodded, then pointed at his monitor. "Someone was in her home, Abe, and had her security code to bypass the system. She said she had only given it to Jordan and her aunt. So who has it and how did they get it?"

Abe stood behind Joseph and read what he had pulled up. "I don't like this, Joseph. Is her keypad visible?"

"No, it's not. I went over the house looking for bugs and didn't find anything. So how did they know?"

"Jordan."

Joseph nodded. "I think we need to look closer at him and also her aunt. I hate to think it would be one of them."

Abe agreed. "Keep searching, Joseph. And give Jace at Tracker's a call and get him looking into their background, Abigail's as well. Something isn't ringing right here."

"No, it's not." Joseph shot a look at the door. "Right now, I think Luke's too close to the situation to read it right."

"He may be. I'll talk with him and get his take on it. I get the feeling he's not comfortable with what she's been saying. Also, get that information to Frankie. He'll need to know that her home has been compromised."

"We have a new team coming in next week, Abe. How do we work that?"

Abe thought about it and then sighed. "I don't know. We need to keep her out of sight. I'll get her set up to do her work from here but that's not going to keep her busy all day and all evening."

Chapter 5

Frankie looked around as he heard his name called and waited for Luke to catch up with him. Luke followed him into Mac's, a local cafe popular with them, and to a booth at the back.

Mac waved and came over with their coffees.

"Thanks, Mac." Frankie reached for the creamers.

"I'll be back with your orders in a few minutes."

Luke shook his head. "I still haven't figured out how he knows what we want."

Frankie shrugged. "He can't tell you either, just that he had this memory for people and food." He stopped, a thought popping up. "I just wonder if those two men were in here for a meal. I wish I had a picture of them."

"Ask him about the voices. Maybe it will ring a bell with him." Luke looked around at the cafe. It wasn't busy, given it was mid-morning. "Abigail talked to her folks yesterday. I think we need to talk to the police department there. She thinks when she would call, that's how she was tracked down."

Frankie nodded. "It more than likely is. But you didn't track me down just for that."

Luke shook his head. "No, I didn't. Joseph checked out her security system. It had been bypassed at some point with the proper code."

"Who all has the code?"

"Jordan and her Aunt Mel. Joseph said it's a good system, shouldn't be easily hacked, and her keypad is situated where it can't be seen. He checked the wiring and didn't see that it had been tampered with." Luke was frustrated. "He also checked for bugs, but didn't find any."

Mac appeared at that moment with their orders. He stood watching the two men, then spoke. "Both of you are troubled. Can I help?"

Luke slid over on the seat so Mac could sit with him. "This may seem a strange question, Mac. Have you had two men in here in the last couple of days, both with gruff voices, one sounding more like a heavy smoker?"

Mac shook his head. "I haven't waited on anyone like that, but I can ask the staff if they have."

"That would be appreciated, Mac." Frankie shared a look with Luke, then spoke. "This is confidential, Mac. If someone can describe a customer like that, we would need to speak with them, in such a way that they aren't put at risk."

"Leave it with me, Frankie, and I'll see what I can find out for you."

Frankie watched him walk away, then spoke. "Knowing Mac, he'll come through with something for us."

Abigail sat back from the computer she was working on, a thought chasing through her mind. She turned, intending to find Luke, and found Micah standing watching her.

"You look like you're headed out on a mission, Abigail."

"I am, Micah. Do you know where Luke is?" She looked past him, hoping to see Luke.

"I think he was headed into Riverville for something. Can I help?"

She studied him. "What's your job with the team, Micah? I know you all have to have a speciality. Luke mentioned that in passing."

"Computers. Why?"

Her face brightened. "Then, you're who I need to speak with." She beckoned him over and pointed at her program. "Something is odd about this program. I know Abe said if I'm working on this it can't be traced, but it seems different than the one at the office."

"Let me sit and I'll take a look." Quickly trading places, Abigail watched as Micah's fingers flew over the keyboard and he brought up different aspects of the program. He stopped at a screen, and she heard a quick intake of breath.

"What did you find?"

"Not what you want to hear. Someone has installed a program in the background of this one. It looks as if it's to pull information from the files. That's not good, Abigail." Micah turned to study her. "Walk me through what you noticed. What's different?"

She shrugged. "I'm not sure. It's just that the program loaded differently than at work. I hardly ever work off site so I can't really tell you what it is."

Micah nodded. "I need to see your computer at the office." He pulled out his phone. "Frankie, it's Micah. Can I get access to the office where Abigail usually works? She's found something off in the program she usually works on. Okay. Thanks. When I figure it out I'll pass it on to your lab techs. They'll need to have access to her computer at home as well as the program she pulled up here at Abe's. What's that? No, there's no way that this can trace her. It's more a program to pull information from the transcripts. Yes, that's very concerning. I would suggest you talk to whoever is in charge and put a halt to any transcription until it's thoroughly investigated."

Abigail watched at Micah pocketed his phone, lost in thought. He looked up at her and blinked.

"Did Joseph give you back your keys?" When she shook her head, he asked, "Do we have your permission to go in and grab your computer? And do you have a laptop you work on?"

"No, just the desktop in the office near the back of the house." She rubbed her hands up and down her arms, suddenly cold. "Is this how they knew where I was?"

Micah shook his head. "Not likely. It would be more from a phone call or email you sent." He stopped and stared at her. "Do you email your parents?"

She shook her head. "No, only phone calls. I don't email anyone, strange as it seems, other than the court reporter's office here. In the past, I never used it, just had it if I ever needed an email."

Micah nodded. "If I have your permission, I'll search your computer as well for anything odd that may mean a tracking program."

"You're scaring me, Micah." Her eyes were troubled.

"I'm sorry, Abigail. I don't mean to. I'm just trying to figure out how they found you." A thought crossed his mind. "Where's your phone?"

"My phone." She turned to head for the bedroom. "It's in my purse. I usually don't hear it ringing though."

Micah was on his feet and walking after her. "If I can see it, I'll check it out as well."

She shook her head. "There are just too many possibilities you're bring up, Micah. How do I stay safe?"

"By working with us and staying here." He watched as she stopped, shook her head, and then walked to the desk where her purse sat. He took the phone she handed him. "Do you ever leave it where someone has access to it?"

"Not usually, though at the office, I have it locked in a desk drawer. I'm in and out of the office some days, but most days, I'm in there for about eight hours working. If I leave at all, I take my purse."

"Thanks, Abigail. I'll check this out and get it back to you." He lifted her phone to wave it at her, then stopped as he studied it. "What's this on the back of it?"

She looked over his hand at it. "I have no idea. I didn't put that there and it wasn't there two days ago when I used it. What is it?"

Micah's face had settled into stern lines. "That is, I think, some kind of a tracking device buried into a sticker. I guess you won't be getting your phone back any time soon. I need to get this to Frankie and the crime lab."

Abigail stepped back, her hands going to her mouth. "A tracking device? But how? When?"

"I'll need you to think back over the last few days and try and remember where and when you had your phone out and if you can, who was around you." Micah looked past her at Luke standing in the doorway. "Luke's here. Talk this through with him."

Micah moved past Luke, stopping for a quick word, then headed for his vehicle. He needed to reach Frankie and quickly. It looked as if whoever was after Abigail knew where she was now.

Luke walked towards Abigail as she stared at him and simply wrapped her in his arms. She clung to him and he felt the shudders going through her. Stepping back, he reached for her hand and pulled her with him to the office.

"Sit, Abigail. Talk to me." Luke knew Abe was behind her at his desk, but she hadn't seen him.

She stared at him, horror in her face. "Is it my fault?" she again asked. "Is it my fault they all died?"

Luke shook his head. "No, it's not. I spoke with Frankie this morning. It wasn't you they were after. It was someone else they think. It wasn't your name that was mentioned. Apparently, there's someone around who looks a little bit like you. But they're still in the early stages of the investigation."

She looked at him, shocked. "Like me?" She shook her head. "I haven't seen anyone who looks like me that works in that office, and I've been working there for a couple of years."

"Think, Abigail. Do you remember hearing about someone who worked there and hasn't for the last couple of years?"

She shook her head. "I don't mingle with the other staff, other than Mary. I go in and out and just do my job. In fact, I couldn't tell you who works there."

"Frankie's looking into that as well. I'm just trying to pick your brain to see if you remember anyone." Luke watched as her brow furrowed in concentration.

"I really don't know of anyone, Luke. They do have turnover." She looked up at him. "Sometimes, they use a temp service if there's a huge backlog. They've been using them pretty constant for the last eight to ten months."

Luke nodded. "Okay, so, where do these work?"

"The office across from me." He heard her words slowing as she realized what she had said. "Is that it? They were looking for someone in that office?"

Luke shrugged as he looked over at Abe. Abe nodded and quietly moved from the room, hand reaching for his phone. He sighed. What next, Lord? Who is going to be a target of these guys? And how do we do this with Abigail? I still feel they were after her.

"We don't know, Abi. Frankie will check all that out." He looked over at the computer she had been working on. "What's this about your computer? I overheard a bit when you and Micah were talking."

She sighed as she turned to look at the computer. "I noticed something off and had Micah look at it. He found a program running in the background of the one I use that picks out information from the transcripts, at least that's what I understood."

"He's gone to talk with Frankie, has he?" At her nod, he continued, "Then, let them work on it. What can we do to make it better for you?"

She stared at him, then shrugged. "Find the guy that did this, Luke, then maybe…" Her voice died away as she stared at him.

"Then, maybe what?"

She shook her head as she rose and headed for the door. "Nothing, Luke, just nothing."

Luke stared after her, a puzzled look in his eyes. What just happened here, Lord? What didn't she say?

Chapter 6

Frankie tracked down the police chief for the town in the break room. He watched for a moment as Caleb Logan stood, mug of tea in hand, and stared at the bulletin board on the wall. He didn't think he was really reading it, not from the look on his face.

"Caleb?"

Frankie's voice brought Caleb back from his thoughts. Shaking his head to mentally come back to the present, he turned to Frankie.

"Where are we at with the investigation, Frankie?"

"Moving very slowly. It's a big investigation, as you know, Caleb. We've had to involve the federal officers as well."

Caleb grimaced at that. "That always goes so well, with their involvement." He motioned towards the door and they walked towards his office. "How is Abigail?"

"Handling it about as well as she can, from what Abe and Micah had said. They have some new information that they've brought in and I've passed it on to the team. Some of it is really disturbing." Seating himself in a chair in front of the desk, he continued. "Micah took a look at the program Abigail usually uses and found a program installed that draws information from the transcripts. He can't say how long it's been there. Our lab techs are looking into that aspect."

"I don't like that. How many trials would have been compromised?" Caleb's keen eyes watched Frankie as he processed that.

"That's a big concern. I've talked to the lead federal investigator and they're looking into that as well. Abigail also says the court reporter's office uses a temp office firm, and that's also being looked at." He sat back, blowing out a breath, watching as Caleb sipped his tea. "There's just so much there, Caleb. All this and the casualties as well and their families. Not to mention Judge Gilmore and his mother."

"Did you ever determine how someone got into her home?"

Frankie shook his head. "Joseph's working that angle but hasn't gotten as far as he'd like. Whoever it was, he said, is good at covering their tracks."

"If he can't find the leak, then they're really good." Caleb looked at the door, then back at Frankie. "How's Luke taking all this?"

Frankie shrugged. "We're not sure. He told them that Abi GG as he calls her was his best friend growing up. I would say he's hurting for her. There's something else going on there as well."

Caleb shook his head. "Keep me updated on it all. I've got all the politicians wanting answers. Our PR team is coming up with new statements all the time." He sat back, his gaze going past Frankie. "I think this is one of the worst cases we have ever had, Frankie, and we've dealt with a lot."

Frankie nodded, then stood. "It is that, Caleb. I'll keep you in the loop."

Caleb watched as he walked away, knowing he'd be looking for Eddie Brown, their top detective. He wished Ben Gray hadn't retired. He had so many contacts from his years. Caleb hesitated, then reached for his phone. Ben still worked for them on occasion. Maybe this would be one of them.

Later that afternoon, Eddie turned from where he was walking away from the department as he heard his name called. Ben and Abe were walking towards him.

"Ben. It's good to see you." Eddie reached to shake his head. "Is this business or pleasure?"

"Business." Ben replied. "Caleb called me in to consult."

"That's the best news I've had today." Eddie shot a look at his nephew, Abe, then commented, "But I don't think you've tracked me down just to say that."

Abe shook his head. "We didn't. Is there some place we can talk?"

"I was heading for Mac's. I'm not going to make it home for Peg's meal tonight, so Mac's is the next best thing."

Mac waved as they headed into the cafe and brought over coffee and mugs. "Are you here for just coffee or a meal?"

"I'm here for a meal, Mac. Can't answer for these two." Eddie doctored his coffee the way he liked it and sipped. As he watched Mac head to the kitchen, he spoke. "All right, Spill. What are you two doing here?"

Ben shook his head. "Caleb's brought me in to consult. He felt I could use my contacts."

"Now, that's the first piece of good news I've heard in the last two days. Glad you're aboard, Ben." Then his eyes turned to his nephew. "Abe, what about you? You're not here for nothing, as you used to say."

"I'm not." He waited as Mac set Eddie's meal in front of him, hesitated a moment, and then left. "Caleb wanted me to talk to you about what we've found so far."

Eddie sliced off a piece of his roast chicken, then pointed his fork at Abe. "What do you have? Frankie's given me all that he has so far."

"Not a whole lot more. Joseph's finally been able to pinpoint when Abigail's security system was breached. It was over a lunch hour." Abe hesitated, not liking what he would have to say next. "We can't account for Judge Gilmore's whereabouts that particular afternoon."

Eddie stopped chewing at that, then swallowed before speaking. "Are you saying what I think I'm hearing?"

Abe nodded reluctantly. "I pray we're wrong, Eddie, but we need to talk to him about that. I just wanted to let you know what Joseph had given us. Abigail is adamant only two others have her security code. Joseph changed it and she hasn't given it to anyone else." Abe paused as his phone vibrated and he pulled it out to look at it. "Now, that's interesting. Someone just tried to use the old code to get into Abigail's house"

"A patrol officer will have responded. Frankie will follow it up. What else?"

Abe shook his head. "There's something else Abigail is working on. I'm not sure if it's clear in her memory or not or how far back it goes."

Ben spoke up. "She may never remember what it was. Fear can do that to a person." He looked around the cafe, which was starting to fill with the supper crowd. "I suggest we do our research and continue on the paths we each have taken on." He was speaking cryptically, but the two men with him caught on.

Ben stood as Abe moved to leave. "Keep us updated, Abe." Sliding back into the booth, he looked over at Eddie and smiled. "I didn't think we'd be working together again on such a big case."

"I didn't either." Eddie's words stopped as he saw Jace from Tracker's heading his way. "Here's Jace, and I don't like the look on his face."

"Eddie. Ben, good to see you." Jace handed over an envelope. "Here's what Tracker and I have come up with so far. This has become a priority with us so we'll keep feeding you what we have as we get it."

Jace was gone before Eddie could say a word. Looking at Ben, he opened the envelope and slid out the papers. He drew a deep breath and looked down at his unfinished dinner. "Let's head back, Ben. This is really interesting material."

Abe thoughtfully pocketed his phone and went on a search. He needed to talk to

Abigail, and he wanted Luke to sit in on the conversation. The information Eddie had just passed on to him was disturbing, to say the least. It put a whole new perspective on what had happened, and it brought the trouble right back to Abigail.

"Luke, got a minute?" Abe tracked him down in the training building. "Where's Abigail?"

Luke looked around. "She was here just a minute ago. Now, where'd she get to?"

"Find her and bring her to the business office. I need to talk to her and I want you there."

Luke shot him a quick look and then headed to find his friend. Who knew where she had gotten to. He didn't like the look on Abe's face.

Chapter 7

"Abi!" Luke's call took Abigail by surprise where she stood looking out over the lake near the back of the cleared area. She turned to watch him stride rapidly towards her, a dark look on his face. Now, what did I do I shouldn't have, she asked herself? Lord, this is getting out of hand. I can't go on like this.

"What's wrong, Luke?" She studied the grim lines on his face and paled. "Who now?"

Luke stopped, mentally kicking himself for scaring her. "No one, Abi. I'm sorry I scared you. Abe needs to talk with you and I didn't know where you had gone. You need to stay close to one of us."

"Even here?" Her hands waved around her. "I thought this was a really safe space."

"It usually is but we've had incidents with intruders. And those intruders have not had the best of intentions." He grasped her hand and pulled her with him at a fast walk. "Just make sure one of us knows where you are, that's all I ask."

Abigail dropped down into a chair near Abe's desk, a disgruntled expression on her face. She glared at Luke, who just stared back at her. Abe bit back a laugh. Luke, my friend, you have your hands full with this one. And I can tell you're not enjoying this one bit, nor is she. Give us a chance to solve this, and then see what happens.

"Abigail." Abe waited for her to turn towards him. When she didn't, he said her name again in a forceful, biting manner. Startled, she looked at him.

"Abigail, don't ever ignore us if we say your name. It could be your life that's at stake. And get that disgruntled look off your face. We're not trying to keep you safe for the fun of it." Abe watched as she struggled with the knowledge he had reminded her of. "Now, Eddie had called me. There is some new information he wants me to run by you."

"Who's Eddie again? I can't keep up with all the names." Abe could see her struggling to remember.

"Eddie is my uncle but more importantly, he's the senior detective on the force and is working with Frankie and a whole team of officers trying to make sense of what has happened. Luke, Ben's been brought in as well."

"Good. He has contacts the others don't have and never will have." Luke settled back against the wall, watchful and alert, arms crossed.

"Caleb has had an investigative team looking into what happened at the courthouse and also with what you've found. It's not pretty what his team is finding. He does have some questions for you about the trials you've been transcribing." As she started to speak, he held up his hand. "We're aware of your confidentiality agreement and we're working around that. We just need general information." He watched as she settled back, eyes narrowed as she stared at the floor. "Have you ever transcribed anything to do with munitions or armaments?"

Her eyes shot to his, round with horror, as she nodded. "I have. There are at least four that I have done. Is this what it's about, Abe?"

Abe shook his head. "We don't know what it's all about yet. It's too early in the investigation for Caleb to even begin to think that way. He's looking at all possibilities. His team is brainstorming for reasons and this was one. This, drugs, murder, your past, your cousin."

"Jordan? How could he be involved?" Abigail was indignant at the thought.

"How about someone tried to get into your place today, with a key, not having the right security code?" Abe watched as she stared back at him, then reality set in.

"Jordan?" She shook her head. "No way, Abe. He wouldn't be involved in anything like this."

"How well do you know him now?" Luke spoke up from where he stood. "How long had it been since you had seen him?"

Abigail turned to look at him, running through her mind. "It's been quite a while, Luke, I would say five to seven years at least before I moved here." She again shook her head. "I don't believe it."

"Then, who all has keys to your house? You told me it was just you, your aunt and Jordan. Are you prepared to say it's your aunt then?" Abe's frustration came through in his voice.

Abigail seemed to shrink before the two men's eyes. Shooting a look at Abe, Luke walked over and crouched beside her chair, reaching for her hand. "We're not saying it's them, Abi. But the investigators have to look at every possibility. Would you rather the questions came from them, from someone you don't know, or from us?"

"You." Her voice was barely audible and Luke could tell the tears were close.

"Ah, Abi GG. Don't cry, please. We're not trying to scare you or tell you that your family is at the bottom of this." Luke reached up to brush away a tear that had escaped. "We just want to keep you safe. Caleb has asked Abe to talk to you and find out what's up. That's all."

She nodded, tears blinding her eyes. "I just don't see them doing that, but Jordan has always been a one-man show. He was away at school, remember, as soon as he could be. Aunt Mel used to talk about how he never would come home unless she ordered him to. She didn't know his friends once he left home. So, it's possible, I guess."

"I remember how worried she was about him and the friends he had during high school. Does she think he ran with the same type of crowd at university?"

Abi nodded. "When I moved here, she told me she hoped that now Jordan would settle down and become like me. I never questioned her. I wish now I had never let Jordan have a key to my house, no matter how much he insisted he had to have."

Abe nodded. "I've sent Joseph and Murphy over to your place. They'll change all the locks and make sure everything is secure. They'll also search through once again to see if they missed anything earlier." He watched as she struggled to comprehend just what was going on. "Caleb has asked that we keep you here for a while. What can we do to make it easier for you?"

She looked up at him and sighed. "I really don't know, Abe. I wish I had my dogs and cat but that's not possible. I wish I could work, but I can't use that program. So, what do I do? Sit around and twiddle my thumbs all day?"

Luke shook his head. "Abi, you're not helping. Abe's trying to make it as easy for you as he can, and you're throwing up roadblocks in front of him. We can't bring you your animals, not yet. I can't take you to see them, not yet anyway. What do you suggest we do with you?"

She sat back, defeat in her body language. "I don't know, Luke. I've been running and on my own for so long. I haven't been able to trust anyone around me. That's coming hard, to let go and let someone else take care of me, to put that much trust in someone."

Abe spoke, compassion flowing through his words. "I understand, Abigail. I know how hard it can be to trust in circumstances you don't understand. Just work with us, okay? Again, what can we do for you that will make it easier?"

She shrugged. "All I know how to do is office work, and you seem to have that under control. I don't read a lot any more, given that I work with words all day. What can I do, Luke? How do I keep busy and my mind off this?"

Luke understood then that she had been running and keeping busy all these years so she couldn't think. His gaze went to Abe and narrowed at the look on Abe's face. What was Abe thinking of now?

"Abigail, you're just what we need." Abe stood and reached for her hand. "Come. You haven't met my sister, Rebecca, yet. She's working on a new photo book but is having trouble with the wording on some of the illustrations and the set up. If you could work with her that would be great. She's in her studio now. Come on, I'll introduce you."

Abigail shot a look of surprise and worry at Luke as he followed them from the office. Abe, he thought, you just might have found something to keep her occupied.

Luke tracked Abe down later that night. "Thanks, Abe. This might just work."

Abe looked up, bringing his mind back to the present. He smiled. "They certainly hit it off, didn't they? I hope it does. We need to keep her occupied so she doesn't try and run on us."

Luke nodded and then studied his friend and team leader. "Are you okay, Abe? You seem a little distracted."

"No, I'm good. Thanks for asking." Abe turned back to his paperwork on the desk in front of him, missing the assessing glance Luke shot at him.

Hearing the door close, and knowing that he was on his own for a bit, Abe sat back. His mind traveled to years earlier and the first day he had met a special lady. He smiled, then his smile grew sad. I wish I knew where you were, my Emma. I wish I knew what he did with you. Brushing his hand across his eyes to clear them of tears, he once again picked up his pen and after a few minutes, concentrated on his paperwork.

Chapter 8

Two days later, Luke and Abigail were in his truck, headed for town. Caleb had asked Luke to bring her in. He had some audio he wanted her to listen to, and he wanted Eddie and Frankie to talk to her again. Luke checked his rearview mirror and nodded. Nathaniel and Matt were in the truck behind him, just for security. Abe was taking no chances.

"What is it again, Luke, that Caleb wanted?"

"He told Abe he has collected some audio he wanted you to listen to. I don't know how many or how he did it." Luke shot her a glance. "It's just an off chance that you might recognize them."

She nodded, her head turned to the window. "How long does it take to find a murderer, Luke?"

"Sometimes months, sometimes weeks, sometimes years." He watched for her reaction.

"Years?" She turned to him in outrage. "There is no way I'm staying here for years."

"No one thinks you will or plans for that to happen. You'll be sprung from our care soon enough."

"Thanks, Luke. You're such a bundle of good news and joy today." She looked away from him, a frown on her face.

"Abi, stop this nonsense. Not one of us likes it either. Where's your faith you're always talking about? Where's your trust in God? The friend I had years ago wouldn't be reacting like this. What happened?"

"Life happened." She turned to look at Luke, then screamed. "Luke, watch out. That truck!"

A sudden sickening crunch of metal drowned out her words as Luke's truck was violently shoved from the road and into the ditch and trees. Silence filled the cab of the truck as the smoke from the deployed airbags floated around the two still forms.

Matt was out of the truck before Nathaniel had brought it to a complete stop. Throwing it into park, Nathaniel followed, stopping to check the truck that had rammed Luke. No driver, he thought, now that's strange. Phone out, he was placing a call to 911 before he was at Luke's door, prying it open. The truck had rammed Luke's just at the mid-point of the vehicle. That's good, Nathaniel thought.

"Can you get in that side, Matt?" Nathaniel listened for Matt's reply as he reached to check Luke, breathing a sigh of relief as he found a pulse. Luke was draped over the steering wheel, and Nathaniel reached to move the airbag away from his face. He looked past Luke at Abigail. She was crumpled against the door and he couldn't reach to her past Luke. He dodged back out and around the truck to find Matt.

"Luke's alive, but I can't get to Abigail."

"I can't get to her either. This way the truck hit, it jammed the frame. These trees are not helping." Matt looked around, frantic to get to the two. "Can we get the back door open on his side?"

Nathaniel nodded. "We can try."

Throwing both of their body weight at the door, they felt it give reluctantly, finally opening enough for Matt to slip in. He reached a shaky hand for Abigail and dropped his head.

"Matt?" Nathaniel's worried question reached him as they heard the sirens approaching.

"She's alive, but her pulse is weak." He moved back out of the truck and then checked Luke. "Thank goodness, help is here."

Matt stood and watched as the town paramedics and firefighters worked to free the two in the truck. Please, Lord, protect them. Heal them. He turned as Nathaniel approached.

"Abe's on his way. He'll call Caleb and let him know what's happened." His eyes too went to his friend. "Any word on how they are?"

Matt shook his head. "Not yet. They're ready to transport Luke. I told them I'd go with Abigail. We need to keep her under our protection. This was planned, Nathaniel."

"I know." Nathaniel stepped to the side to study the path of the truck, his eyes tracing back to the top of the hill the truck had traveled from. "They have had to known we were on our way in and when we left the compound. This was rigged. That truck had picked up a fair amount of speed by the time Luke was passing."

Matt nodded, as he watched the ambulance carrying Luke move away, police escort in place. "I don't like this, Nathaniel.

Who knew? This wasn't arranged until an hour ago. How did they know and get this arranged in time?"

Nathaniel nodded. "There's a leak somewhere, Matt, and not on our side. I would hate to think it's one of Caleb's guys."

Matt turned as he heard footsteps approaching. Abe stood beside them, darkness covering his face as he studied the two trucks.

"Talk to me, guys. What happened?"

"That's what we've been trying to figure out, Abe. That truck came out of that side road with enough speed to do what it did. There was no driver." Abe's eyes shot to Nathaniel. "It was rigged to hit him."

"How did they know?" Abe's question echoed theirs.

"That's what I want to know. None of us knew we were heading into town until an hour ago. So, where's the leak?"

Abe nodded grimly. "That's what I'll be asking Caleb." He turned to look back towards their home area. "If they had the truck up there with a man waiting and someone watching the compound, it could be done. But how would they have known to be up there today?"

Matt walked towards the paramedics as they lifted the stretcher with Abigail on it into the ambulance and spoke quietly to the head paramedic. The man nodded and Matt climbed in beside her.

"Who lets her cousin and aunt know?" Nathaniel's question caught Abe's attention, and he turned to stare at his friend.

"Caleb, I think, or Eddie or Frankie. We want someone high up that can read his reaction."

Nathaniel stared at Abe, then back at the truck. "You don't think he had anything to do with this, do you?"

"Right now, I'm open to any and all suggestions. Come on, Nathaniel. Let's head into town."

Abe paced the waiting room of the local hospital Emergency Department. How many times had he done just that in the recent past, he couldn't quite remember. He turned and searched the area. His team were all there, in uniform and armed, worry evident on their faces. He looked further and found Abigail's aunt sitting by herself, shredding the tissue she held in her hands. Abigail's cousin wasn't there. Abe knew he didn't have to be in a courtroom that day. So, where was he? Abe turned as he heard footsteps approaching. Caleb and Frankie stood beside him.

"Any word yet, Abe?" Caleb's voice was hushed, but angry.

"Not yet. John Thompson was out about half an hour ago and spoke with Abigail's aunt. We haven't had any word on Luke yet."

Caleb nodded, then looked around. "We need to talk, Abe." He was hesitant to continue. "We can't find Judge Gilmore."

"What? How can that be?" Abe stared at his friend. "Isn't he under protection?"

"He is and somehow slipped away from his security team. I can tell you, heads are rolling on the federal side over this. Jace did some digging for us. The Judge's friends during university were just on the right side of the line and many suspect often slipped over the line."

"Abigail said her aunt was worried about him. Apparently he ran with a group like that in high school." Abe turned as he heard his name called. A nurse stood near him.

"Mr. Finlay, if you'll come this way, the doctor wishes to speak with you."

"Go ahead, Abe." Eddie's voice came from behind him. "We'll wait."

Abe could see his team members standing alert and watchful. He knew prayers would be going up but just how to pray, he wondered? How serious are these injuries?

He followed the nurse to one of the rooms, hesitating as she opened the door. A smile of compassion from her sent him in. John Thompson was standing at Luke's side, stethoscope to his chest. He glanced up at Abe, then concentrated once more on his assessment.

When he straightened back up, he stood for a minute, staring down at Luke.

"John? How is he?" Abe was almost afraid to ask.

John shot him a keen eyed look. "He's hurting, Abe, as you would expect. Nothing broken. The impact and the deployment of the airbags knocked him out. He's got some burns on his hands and face from the chemicals. A concussion for sure. Bruises, cuts from the glass. God had His hand on those two. If the truck had hit further to the front, we wouldn't be having this conversation."

Abe nodded. "I get that, John. How long will you keep him in?"

John shrugged. "A day if he'll stay. Knowing him, he'll discharge himself as soon as he can." John turned and motioned for Abe to follow him. "I understand from Caleb that your team is providing security for Abigail Gilmore?" At Abe's nod, he continued, "She's here in the next room. Your man, Matt, has refused to leave her side, no matter where we've taken her."

"He's correct, John. She's under our care after that incident the other day. That I'm telling you so that as her physician you understand why we need someone with her. One of my team will be in the room at all times. Caleb's providing an officer for the door. Now talk to me about her injuries. I know I'm not next of kin but we can't get them here."

John nodded. "That's okay. She was awake for a bit and told me to tell you. She's fortunate as well. About the same as Luke only her right shoulder is damaged. We're taking her to the operating room in a bit to set it and the upper arm bone. Other than that she's fine."

"When can we take her out of here?" Abe was worried. It would be too easy, even with security in place, for someone to get to her.

"Tomorrow, I think, if she's okay after the surgery. Your man, Matt, is good. I'll have Mary head out for a couple of days as well." Mary, his wife, was a trained nurse and John often had her step in for home care on patients when they were released from the hospital.

Abe nodded. "That's good." He turned to head away. "Warn your people that IDs will be checked. One of my team will be with each of them at all times. Assign only one nurse to the both if you can. No cleaning staff. If you need lab work, have the nurse with them."

John nodded. "I'll see to that, Abe. I get what you're not saying."

Chapter 9

Abe stood in the doorway of his spare bedroom and watched as Matt and Nathaniel settled Luke into the bed. Luke was in pain, Abe could tell, and was refusing pain medications. He knew he'd have to step in soon, but he prayed Matt would get Luke to take something.

Luke laid back on the pillows and closed his eyes. He didn't think he had ever hurt this much, but he was reluctant to take any medications. What he wanted was to see Abigail, and that they weren't letting him do. He drifted off, not knowing that John Thompson had given him something before he left for the pain and as a sedative. John knew him too well.

Nathaniel turned at a question from Matt and nodded. He wasn't leaving the room just yet. John had asked someone to sit with Luke for a few hours, just to be on the safe side.

Abe stepped aside as Matt came back through the door. "How is he, Matt, other than sore?"

"Mad that this happened and he couldn't prevent it. He's fighting taking the pain meds, but John said he gave him something earlier. Nathaniel's staying with him for now."

Abe nodded, then looked at the closed doorway to the next room. "And Abigail? Mary getting her settled in?"

Matt nodded. "I'm going to check on her and make sure Mary has everything she needs." He stopped, a look of anger and frustration crossing his face. "Who did this, Abe? Are we any closer to finding out? We need Luke on training next week, and now we don't have him."

Abe agreed. "We'll work around it, Matt. There are some things we offer in training that we don't need to. His will be one that we don't offer this course. The trainees understand coming in that not everything we offer is provided in a week. We just can't do it all. I think Abe and Caleb will be wanting to speak with you and Nathaniel when he's free. I left them in my office."

Matt nodded, his hand on the door knob. "I'll be along as soon as I can."

Caleb looked up as Abe entered his office and crossed to drop heavily into his desk chair. Abe is wearing thin, Caleb thought. How much more can he take?

"How are they, Abe?" Eddie's voice cut through Caleb's thought.

"They're hurting. Luke is fighting any pain medications. Abigail didn't stir at all as she was moved. John had made sure she had as much pain medication as he thought she could handle before we brought her out here. Mary's getting her settled now." He looked towards the doorway. "Matt will be here shortly. Nathaniel's with Luke for now, but Murphy's heading that way soon. Both will be here to talk with you about yesterday." He scrubbed his hands down his face. "Was it only yesterday?"

The two men facing him saw the fatigue and worry in his face. Abe usually hid his emotions, but today he wasn't able to.

"Did you talk to her family, Caleb?" Abe's question caught him off guard.

"I did. They wanted to head this way, but agreed not to when I told them it was too dangerous. Her mom, especially, is hurting that she can't be here."

Abe nodded. "Where do we stand right now, Caleb? How close are we to finding these guys?"

Caleb blew out a breath of frustration. "No where close to finding them, Abe. I was hoping Abigail might recognize those voices, but that's off for now."

"What about her cousin?"

Eddie shook his head. "We haven't been able to find him. The federal authorities are working that one. We did get permission from her aunt to go through his home. We found some interesting items, between the feds and us."

Abe nodded, then looked up as Nathaniel and Matt entered.

"Caleb, you wanted to talk to us?" Nathaniel's voice was quiet even for him.

"We did, guys. Sit. This may take a bit." Caleb studied the two men as they sat. This was taking a part of them as well. "I just wanted to go back over yesterday. I know the patrol officers took your statements, but seeing as it happened while you were working security, I wanted to ensure that nothing was missed."

Nathaniel and Matt exchanged looks.

"We've been going back over what we saw. Unfortunately it just happened so quick." Matt closed his eyes as he replayed the scene. "I can't think of anything I saw or felt that I didn't say."

Nathaniel agreed. "Did you find out whose truck it was?"

Eddie nodded. "It was stolen three days ago."

"Three days? Where was it then, up there?"

Caleb nodded. "It's entirely possible. I suspect you were watched at the courthouse, Nathaniel, and someone figured out that Abigail would be here, under guard. They've been watching for an opportunity."

Abe spoke up. "I had some of the team go out and look around up there. They found evidence, once again, that we were being watched, but nothing to connect it to the truck."

"We didn't find evidence where the truck was or in the truck itself. That's where we stand, fellows." To say Caleb was beyond frustrated would be an understatement.

Abe headed back to his office once the four men had scattered. He needed to spend some time in prayer, but something was bothering him, and bothering him a lot, about what happened. Why was Abigail a target? It didn't make sense if it was because of what she had transcribed. The court cases were already settled. And that program Micah had found. That didn't make a lot of sense either.

Lord, we could use Your help about now, he prayed. We're at a loss as to who and why. Guide our search to the right ones.

He stopped and stared around the room, not sure what he was looking for. Then he walked towards the book shelf, the reminder of a book pulling him that way. He found it and returned to his desk, leafing through it.

Chapter 10

A tap at his door hours later brought his head up from his notes. Luke stood there, shaky but upright. Abe stood and went towards him, then watched as he walked in and sank into one of the arm chairs, sighing as he did so.

"Should you be up?"

Luke nodded. "I needed to get up, Abe. I can't lie around while you are all trying to figure out who and why."

"You need time to heal, Luke. It's only going to get worse before you feel better."

Luke cracked an eye open at that and glared at Abe. "Thanks for the reminder." Abe smiled, then sat back at his desk. "What are you working on, Abe?"

Abe held up the paperback book he had been reading. "This. It's a novel that was popular a few years ago, *It's All About Me.* Some things about what we're going through sounded a little too familiar."

"Are you saying someone is following a plot line?" Luke was in disbelief.

Abe rose and handed over the book to Luke, then sat in the chair beside him. "I'm not saying that. It's just a little too much like one of the story lines in there." He looked around, then back at Luke. "I have Jace working on tracking down who the author is. A friend recommended it to me as a resource for security. He was right."

Luke read the synopsis on the back, then looked over at Abe. "Are you saying someone wrote this and is now playing it out for real?"

Abe nodded. "That's the way it's feeling, but I can't be sure. Whoever the author is, he or she has covered themselves with layers of protection. Not just, I'll take a pseudonym for writing. I'm hoping Jace can track it down."

As he spoke, his phone chimed. "Speaking of Jace. Jace, what do you have? I see." Abe's eyes shot to Luke, who was studying the book. "Now that's interesting. Email Frankie with that will you, or Eddie? This may be the link we're looking for. Thanks again."

Luke looked up as Abe thoughtfully stuffed his phone back into his pocket. "What did he find?"

"Guess who our author is?"

"Either the judge or his mother."

"How about both - a joint effort?"

Luke stared at Abe, then out the doorway towards the bedrooms. "Does Abi know that?"

"Not likely. Now this is very concerning. We need to make sure her aunt doesn't have any contact with her. I'll have one of you guys pick up her animals and bring them out here. It will help keep her occupied and happy while she's healing."

"Did John say how long it would be? I haven't really heard how bad she was." Luke pretended low concern, but his heart hurt that his friend was injured on his watch.

Abe watched as Luke tried hard to hide his feelings. Something more than friendship is going on here, Lord, and it stretches back many years. "John said she was like you— bruises, cuts, some chemical burns on the face from the airbags. She did have to have surgery to repair her broken shoulder and upper arm."

Luke's eyes shot to Abe's, and then slid closed. "I didn't see the truck, Abe. I didn't see it in time to prevent this."

"That was the whole point, Luke. It was staged in such a way you couldn't. Caleb's team has added that to their list for investigation, but unfortunately, they don't have much in evidence to work on right at the moment."

Luke stood, shaky for a minute, then started to pace. "What can we do, Abe? How do we keep her safe?"

"She'll be staying put for a few weeks with her injuries. That's almost a blessing in disguise. I hope by the time she's well enough for physiotherapy, we'll have found the culprits."

Luke stopped his pacing, thoughts racing through his mind. "I still can't see her aunt and cousin writing that book. It doesn't fit with what I remember." He shrugged. "But then it's likely 15 years since I've seen her aunt, and longer than that for her cousin. People can change." He turned to head for the door. He was exhausted, but wanted to check on Abigail again.

"Luke." Abe's voice from behind him stopped him. When Abe didn't speak again, he turned. "Just so you know, we'll do our best to keep your lady safe." Luke frowned at him, trying to understand what he was saying. Abe laughed. "She's your lady, Luke. You just haven't gotten to that point."

Luke nodded. "She is and I have. I just don't know if she has."

Luke turned to leave again as Abe's soft comment reached him.

"She has, Luke. She's just waiting for you."

Abe pulled his phone from his pocket as he moved to the door to watch Luke. "Finlay. Jace? That was quick? What's that? Are you sure? Okay, get it to Eddie or Frankie. I'm on my way there."

Joseph stopped Abe on his way to his truck. "We've got Abigail's dogs and cat. Ashling Bradley took them. The thing is it was very weird."

Abe stopped, a question in his eyes. "What do you mean?"

"There was no one home. The dogs were tied up in the back yard, with their dishes and food. The cat was in its carrier on the back deck, same with the food and dishes."

Abe shook his head. "That's about what I figured. Listen, Joseph, warn the team we need to stick close to Luke and especially Abigail. I don't like that Mary's here, but we need her. I just found out that both her aunt and cousin are missing and that they were instrumental in writing a book, whose plot line we seem to be following somewhat."

"A plot line?" Joseph shook his head. "I'll let the guys know. And we'll be armed from now on in."

"Good. I'm off for a meeting with Caleb and Eddie over what Jace has pulled up. I'm not sure what time I'll be back. Luke's been up but he needs to be lying down again. Get Matt to make sure he does."

Luke looked up as Mary stopped beside him, laying a hand on his shoulder. "You need to go rest, Luke. I can see the pain in your face."

He shook his head, and she looked behind him at Matt and Murphy, a pleading look on her face. The two men approached and hauled him to his feet.

"Come on, Luke. Let's get you to your bed. You're not doing anyone any good like this." Murphy kept his hand on Luke's arm to steady him.

Matt waited for Mary to speak. "Thank you. I couldn't get him to leave."

Matt shook his head. "No, I didn't think you would be able to. If you need anything, Mary, let us know." Matt took a look at Abigail lying still on the bed, and then to the door where Luke had exited. "Abe wanted me to warn you. The authorities are looking for her aunt and her cousin right now. Our team will be around and armed at all times. Don't hesitate to call if you need someone. One of us will be in the house at all times and two of us outside for the duration."

Mary looked shocked, then her face smoothed out. "Thank you, Matt. It's good to know. But God has His hand in this as well. That's where our trust in Him comes in."

"That it does, Mary."

Caleb looked up as Eddie, Frankie and Abe appeared in his doorway. He sighed, knowing that he wasn't going to get out of there early as he had hoped.

"What do you have. Eddie?"

"Not what you're going to want to hear, Caleb. Both Abigail's aunt and cousin are now missing. Abe's come up with some thoughts and Jace check them out."

Caleb sat back, watching as the men seated themselves. "What do you have?" He reached for the paperwork Frankie handed him and read. "Is this for real?"

Abe nodded. "It is. Jace is still working through some of it for us, but what you have is what he's got so far." He paused, then continued. "When Joseph went to get Abigail's pets, they were all in the back yard. No sign of any other life that they could see."

"So, both are on the run?" Caleb looked over at Frankie. "You're on that?"

Frankie nodded. "We are. So far, no hits on the vehicles or their credit or debit cards."

"Make sure our team gets this and works it through. Have Sue get in touch with Jace and pick his brain." He looked at the three men. "This is not getting any easier, is it? Abe, you're on their security?"

Abe nodded. "I am. My men are all armed now and taking shifts for protection. Next week, we have a team coming in for training, but that training is going to change in tone. It's known that we offer lots of different training. Next week, it will be specialized to a couple of areas. It's in the contract, so no one can complain."

They stood to leave, then Caleb called Abe back. "How are the two feeling tonight, Abe?"

"Luke seems to be getting back on his feet. He'll be hurting for a few days, likely. Mary said Abigail had been awake a couple of times, just enough to get some fluid into her, and then back to sleep. She's been under heavy pain medication."

"Keep my updated and let me know what we can do to help. A patrol car will be out your way more often over the next few days. The feds wanted to move in and take over security, that is, until they found out how high your clearances are."

Abe laughed. "That always works, doesn't it?"

Chapter 11

Early morning, Abigail stirred, trying to turn over, but stopping, the pain from her shoulder bringing her wider awake. She searched the room in the early morning light and sighed. She wasn't in the hospital. Thank you, Lord. I don't think I could have stayed there much longer. She sensed a presence to her left and looked up.

"Mary Thompson! What are you doing here?"

"Looking after you, my dear. How are you this morning?" Mary brushed the hair back from Abigail's eyes and assessed her at the same time. The pain was still there, Mary thought, but not as intense.

"I feel like I was run over by a truck. No, I guess that should be run into by a truck. Did they catch the driver?" When Mary didn't respond, Abigail looked up and groaned. "No driver, right? I didn't think I saw one."

"No, no driver. Caleb's wanting to talk with you at some point, but it can wait. Do you want to sit up a bit more?"

Abigail winced with pain as she moved. "What happened to me, Mary?"

"A fractured shoulder and upper arm, which they had to set in surgery. You'll be laid up for a while."

Abigail's face pulled into a grimace of pain and frustration. "That's not what I wanted to hear."

"No, I didn't think it would be. Once I've washed off your face, I'll put on some more of the cream. You have some burns from the airbag chemicals, assorted bumps, bruises and some cuts. A mild concussion to top it off."

"How's Luke?" Abigail wouldn't look up as she asked, her heart was too open and in her eyes.

Mary studied her young friend and nodded. Abe was right. Dear Lord, bring these two through their troubles and to each other. "He doesn't have any broken bones, but other than that, what I said to you applies to him." She stepped back to reach for the medications Abigail needed and paused at the look on the younger woman's face. "Abigail, what is it?"

Abigail sighed. "I just want my Mom and I know she's not able to be here. It's too dangerous for her." Tears she wasn't able to control dripped down her face.

Mary sat and drew Abigail into a hug. "I know, dear. It doesn't matter how old we are, when we're sick or hurting, it's only our Moms who can make us feel better."

Luke tapped at the partially open door and then peeked in. Mary looked up at him and then down at Abigail. Abigail wasn't ready for Luke to see her yet. Luke took another look and moved on to search for Abe.

"Abe, where are we in the investigation, do you know?"

Abe turned from the window he had been staring out of and looked back at Luke. "Not where we would like to be, Luke. Her aunt and cousin are missing, Caleb's crew are going over the truck again, but we don't have anything yet that would lead us to the perpetrators."

Luke was frustrated. He and Abigail had been hurt, someone had tried to abduct her, and they had nothing. "That's not what I wanted to hear."

"I know. It's going to take a lot of prayer, my friend. Come, let's get some food into you." Abe waited as Luke hesitated, then turned for the kitchen. "Mary's looking after getting something for Abigail. Your lady will be up and about soon."

Luke's footsteps stopped at Abe's last sentence, and then he nodded. She would be, but was she really his lady?

Frankie looked up from the myriad of paperwork on his desk at the tap on his door. Jake Wilson, the patrol officer who had responded to the wreck, stood there, still in his coveralls from going back over the trucks. An evidence bag was in his hand.

"What do you have there, Wilson?" Frankie frowned as he extended a hand to take it from Wilson.

"You're not going to like this, Frankie. We went over the truck at the scene, we went over it when we brought it in, and I went back over it this morning. I found that this morning, sitting on the passenger seat of the suspect truck. It wasn't there before."

Frankie's gaze froze on Wilson as he took in what was being said. Then he looked down at the note. "Not another one aimed at Abe? What is it with this guy?"

Wilson shook his head. "So who was the accident aimed at, Abigail or Abe, or both?"

Frankie stared across the room. "That's an interesting question, Wilson. You say this was just there this morning?" At Wilson's nod, he continued. "I want the names of everyone who had access to the garage in the last twenty-four hours and I want that list taken to Tracker's. Include your own, Wilson. We need to find out who placed this note. The cameras were working?"

Wilson turned to look behind him. "That's what I'm looking into next. Do you want me back on patrol or on this?"

"On this." Frankie stared down at the note, then back up at Wilson. "Put in your request for transfer to detectives, Wilson, if that's what you want. I'll make sure it goes through. We can use you in this department."

Wilson looked taken aback, then nodded. "Thank you, Frankie. You'll have it on your desk today."

"As of now, Wilson, I'll clear it with Eddie and Caleb to have you working full time with us on this investigation."

Wilson nodded and headed away as Frankie stood. He headed for Eddie and then Caleb. Neither would be happy with what Frankie had in his hand.

"It was where?" Caleb studied the note, then looked up at Frankie.

"On the seat in the suspect truck. Wilson found it this morning. He's compiling a list of everyone who had access to the garage, including himself."

Caleb sighed. "Which one of you want to talk to Abe?"

Eddie looked up from the photo he had taken. "I will. I need to talk to him anyway." He took a look at Frankie, then at Caleb. "Have we any word on the cousin or aunt?"

Frankie shook his head. "They've disappeared. We obtained the warrants we needed to go through their homes. They're not the innocents that Abigail thinks they are. We found evidence that her cousin is deep into smuggling and we're tracking what that was. Her aunt seems to be involved as well, from the documents we've found. Our computer techs are going over their home computers. We've also searched his court office and taken his computer from there.

"Caleb, I told Wilson to put in for that empty spot on the detectives and pulled him from patrol to help with this."

Caleb stared at Frankie for a minute, his mind going over Wilson's record. "That's a good plan. He'll do well. Which tow company brought in the trucks?" he asked as a thought hit him.

"Joseph's Leah for Luke's and Smitty for the suspect one." Smitty's was a well-known tow company and his daughter, Leah, worked for him.

"Then we don't have to worry about any evidence tampering on the tow in. It has had to be someone on the force." Caleb sat back. "There have been no civilians in there right?"

Frankie shook his head. "No, we made sure only police personnel had access, and now we have this. Who did he reach?"

Abe looked back as he crossed to his business office. Eddie had driven in and was approaching him. Lord, please, let there be good news for a change. We need it so much. Luke and Abigail are healing physically but emotionally they're both hurting.

"Eddie, what brings you out?"

"Abe, we need to talk and talk seriously." Eddie pointed towards the office building. "Is your office free?"

Abe nodded and led the way, sinking down into his chair. "I don't like the look on your face, Eddie."

Eddie simply handed over the envelope he had been carrying. "Read this and we'll talk."

Abe reached for the envelope. "Another one, Eddie?"

"Tsk, tsk, tsk, Finlay. You'll never learn will you? How many men, how many injuries or even death?"

"Where'd this come from?"

Eddie watched Abe for a minute, then commented, "That's the interesting thing, Abe. Wilson found it on the suspect truck seat this morning."

Abe's eyes shot to his uncle's. "This morning? Why didn't they find it before?"

"Because it wasn't there before," Eddie replied. "Wilson's working on who it was."

"This has never made any sense, Eddie. I have no idea who this would be."

Eddie nodded. "I know you don't and I know the guys understand that. This time, though, it was a lot worse."

Abe nodded. "I know. I just can't put a finger on who it would be."

Eddie stood. "If you do, let me know."

Abe watched as his uncle walked away, then turned back to the note, looking up as Murphy spoke.

"Another note, Abe?"

Abe nodded and handed over the picture. "Another one, Murphy, and I am no closer to knowing who it is or why."

"We get that, Abe. We know you well enough to understand that if you knew you'd be all over this guy."

Abe nodded and then turned the conversation to work.

The watcher stood once more up in the hills, staring down at the compound. Soon, he thought. Soon, I'll have him where I want him and he'll tell me what I want to know. He took one more look, then turned and walked away.

Chapter 12

To say that Abigail was tired of her life as she now lived it would be a huge understatement. She chafed under the weight of the bandages and cast, of the inability to do much, of not being able to work. Luke took one look at her about a week after their accident, then went looking for Abe.

"Abe, where do they stand on the investigation?" Luke dropped down into the seat in front of Abe's desk.

Abe looked up, drawing his thoughts back from the distant past. "I haven't heard in the last couple of days, Luke, but they haven't made much headway."

"No signs of her aunt or cousin?"

Abe shook his head. "They've gone into hiding. Frankie's still looking for a connection between what Abigail saw and what happened a few weeks ago. There's something there, he's sure, but he can't prove it."

"Has Jace come up with anything?"

Abe shook his head. "He's working on it but had to set it aside for a few days. He's waiting for some information to come back, he told Frankie." Abe sat back and studied Luke. "Now, what can we do to help Abigail?"

Luke shrugged. "I'm really not sure, Abe. I've been trying to come up something. We need to get her out of here for a few hours, I think, just to give her a chance of scenery. She's due to go into tomorrow for her checkup."

Abe nodded. "How she's feeling other than caged?"

"Physically, she's still hurting. Mary says she's not sleeping well either." Luke looked around, frustrated that he couldn't fix it for his friend. "I just wish I knew who, Abe."

"We all do, Luke." Abe looked over as a knock came at the door, and Jace peeked in. "Jace? What are you doing out here?"

"Tracker came through, Abe. She found some stuff she wanted you to have right away. I'm dropping off a copy at the department as well."

"Sit. What kind of information sends you out?"

Jace handed over the envelope he had been carrying. "You're not going to like what we've found, Abe, nor will Abigail."

"That sentence doesn't bode well for what you're handing me."

"No, it doesn't. I don't know how Tracker found that information, but she has a memory like I've never seen for people and places. When you passed on the town and date, she dug that up."

Luke watched, frown in place, as Abe pulled out the documents, read them and then passed them over.

"Her cousin is involved in that as well?"

Jace nodded. "He used an alias but his face was recognized. They did get fingerprints but they're not his. They haven't been able to track them down."

"Anything else, Jace?"

Jace nodded, a grim look on his face. "I've been talking to my street sources here and in Oak City. There's a contract out on Abigail, Abe, not connected to that murder. It's connected to something else. My sources are being very quiet as to what it is, but I'm still digging."

Luke stopped reading at that, and looked first at Abe, then at Jace. "A contract? Is that what they were after that day?"

Jace nodded. "From what I'm told it is. What I'm getting is that it's related to her cousin. He's a bit of nasty work."

Luke agreed. "I never liked him. Her aunt, now she always presented herself differently than her cousin."

"You may know what the material is, Luke, given your specialty. I'm hearing munitions or armaments or bomb making material being smuggled into the area somewhere."

Abe froze. "Bomb making material. Any word on a target?"

Jace shook his head. "Not that I've been told, but there are a lot of celebrations upcoming and it could be any one of those."

"Caleb needs to hear this. You're headed that way?"

Jace stood. "I am. Luke, keep your friend out of sight and safe. I'm working on trying to get photos of the men involved, and when I do, you'll get a copy. Abe, I have your secure email. I'll send on what I discover. I just thought you needed to hear it from me."

"I did. Thanks, Jace, and give our thanks to Tracker."

Jace shrugged. "She won't let me say a word of that to her. She never does. She does what she has to and moves on to the next task. She doesn't want to hear thanks from our clients, preferring not to know who they are."

Luke watched him leave, then glanced back at the papers he held. "Where now, Abe? How do we keep her safe?"

Abe nodded. "I know, Luke, I know. I have no idea at present, and I don't think she'll go along willingly with any plans we make."

"No, I don't think she will. She wouldn't in the past. Now, I'm not so sure. She's changed in the last few years." Luke stared down at the papers he held. "I just don't understand, Abe, how her family got into this."

Abe reached for the papers and read through them again, pausing at a name. "What was her uncle's name?"

"William. Why?"

Abe tapped the papers with his forefinger. "He started it off, forty years ago."

"What?" Luke was shocked. "But he had a hardware store in town and never traveled."

"Very handy cover, that of a hardware store. Who would question deliveries coming in at any hour?"

Luke sat back, deep in thought. "I guess we'll need to talk to her. I don't like the thoughts of how she'll take it."

A tap at the door paused the conversation, and then Abigail peeked in. "Am I disturbing anything?"

The men shot each other a look, then Luke rose and went to draw her into the office. He gently shoved down into his chair and then sat beside her. "Actually, we were just talking about you. Something's come up that we need to bring up with you."

Abigail looked between the two of them. "Why do I feel that I'm not going to like this?"

Abe leaned forward, arms on his desk. "I don't think you will, but it's something we have to address, sooner than later."

"I can tell I'm not going to like it, Abe, so why don't you just speak up and tell me?" Abigail faced him straight on, eyes refusing to drop.

Abe sighed, looked at the paperwork Luke held, and then said, "How well did you know your uncle?"

"William?" At his nod, she shrugged. "He was a hard man to get to know, a hard man any way you wanted to put it. I never felt comfortable around him. Why?"

"Jace, from Tracker's, a local investigative firm, has come up with some new information for us. Your uncle was involved in smuggling: bomb components, weapons."

Abigail nodded. "I knew it. I always thought there was something odd about the deliveries he was getting, but when I asked Aunt Mel, she just shrugged it off and said that was how business worked. If that was the case, why was it only him? He had the perfect cover, you know."

Abe and Luke looked at each other. This was not the reaction they had expected.

"Did you ever talk to anyone else?" was Abe's next question.

"I was young when he died and didn't talk to anyone. They would have put it off as the imagination of a child."

"More than likely. We know differently now, Abi." Luke reached for her good hand and grasped it tight. "We believe you. Now, do you remember anything else?"

"Let me think about it and I'll see what I can remember. You're thinking dates, people, if I saw any goods?"

Abe nodded. "We also need to find out how deep your aunt and cousin were."

"Knowing what I know now, I would say very deep. Jordan worked in the store all the time, and Aunt Mel did too. There's no way they didn't know what was going on." She stared at the hand Luke had in his. "How far does this go, Abe, and how is it related to what happened in the courthouse?"

"That's what Frankie and Eddie are working on. They'll get to the bottom of it."

"But who has to die before they do?" Abigail pulled her hand away from Luke and stood. "Is there anyway that I can stay in town for a bit tomorrow after my appointment? I would like to wander some shops, go to Mac's, just do something other than sitting around?"

Abe nodded, knowing how caged she had been feeling. "Let me work on that. It means that more than Luke would be with you, but we'll get you some time, Abigail."

"Thank you, Abe." She stopped, staring at the floor, then raised her eyes. "This is when it's so hard to trust, to know that God has plans and purposes already in place." She turned and walked away.

They watched her walk away. "How long, Abe? How long can we keep her safe?" Luke expressed the thoughts of them both.

"As long as we can. Now about tomorrow, who do we send with you?"

Chapter 13

Murphy and Joseph sat in the waiting room at the hospital, watching the activity around them. They had no idea the clinic would be so busy.

"I wish we could have had a better time for Abigail to be here." Joseph's words echoed Murphy's thoughts.

"I do too. When she comes back the next time, we'll have to work it out differently. There are just too many people here."

Joseph nodded. "I don't like it, Murphy. It's too easy for someone to get to her." Looking over towards the reception desk, he tapped Murphy's arm and then rose. "Let's see when she's next due to come in and request, no demand, the first one of the day."

Abigail was tired and sore. The poking and prodding on her shoulder had hurt, as had when the stitches had been pulled. She looked up as Joseph and Murphy approached.

"When are you due to come back, Abigail?" Joseph's question caught her attention.

"Two weeks. Why?"

Joseph turned to the secretary. "We need the first appointment of the day."

"Well, that's just not possible. It's already taken." The woman looked him up and down.

"No, we get the first appointment of the day. It is really a matter of life and death for this woman." Luke spoke up, his voice firm with an underlying tension in it that stopped the woman. "If we have to, we'll gladly speak with the physician and request an appointment before your clinic starts. Now, what will it be?"

She looked flustered and saw the physician approaching.

He spoke. "Give them an appointment before the clinic opens. You don't have to be here, I can see to them myself." He turned and walked away, leaving her with her mouth open in protest.

"Fine. Here." She almost threw the appointment card at them.

"In future, I would suggest you keep your temper in control. You have no idea what is at stake with this lady. The physician does. If you want me to put in a complaint about your attitude, I can do that." Luke stared at her until she looked down. With that, they turned and walked away, Abigail between them.

They walked through the parking lot to Joseph's truck, eyes watchful, Abigail between them as much as they could get her. As Luke helped her into the truck, she spoke. "Is this really necessary?"

The three men shared a glance, then Luke replied, "It is, Abi. We have no idea when they'll try again to get you."

She sat back as Luke pulled the seat belt over and fastened it for her, then climbed in himself. "When does it end, guys?"

"Hopefully soon. We need to catch the guys after you." Murphy took a look back at her, then glanced at Luke, who nodded.

"Where now, Abi? Do you still want to wander some shops?"

She shook her head. "No, I don't think I do. I wouldn't mind stopping at Mac's if we could."

"That we can do, Abigail." Joseph spoke as he headed that way. "I think we can manage to get you a meal out in safety."

Abigail slid awkwardly across the seat as Luke followed her into one of the booths at the back of Mac's. Murphy slid in opposite them. Mac waved and headed for the kitchen, knowing what they would want. Joseph stopped for a minute at the front of the cafe, assessing the patrons, then joined the three.

Abigail finally set down the part of a burger she had been eating, eyes sparkling with humour. The three men had done their best to lift her spirits. "Listen, you three. I've had enough. Now eat."

"Yes, ma'am." Joseph laughed at her frown. Then eyes narrowing, he excused himself. Murphy watched him walk out of the cafe towards his vehicle.

What's up, he wondered, then watched at Luke excused himself to talk to Mac. As they waited, a large heavyset man suddenly sat in Luke's spot. Abigail's eyes flew to Murphy as she crowded herself further from the man.

"You're coming with us, young lady."

She began shaking her head. "No, I'm not."

Murphy heard the click of a safety being released and knew that the man had a gun hidden under the table and pointed directly at him.

"I have a weapon pointed at your friend here. It's nothing to me if he dies now or later. So, you two are going to rise and walk out ahead of me."

Murphy caught a glimpse of a truck moving slowly in the parking lot and then stopping. His mind racing as to how they could get out of there, he saw Luke cautiously approaching, then noticed that Mac was moving the patrons out of the restaurant very quietly and quickly, taking them out past the kitchen. Good, he thought. Now, how do we get Abigail out of here?

The man pointed at him. "All right, up you get. Now! I really don't care if you die here or later. It's the woman we want." He stopped as he felt a touch of metal at his ear.

"I don't think so." Luke's voice was grim and quiet. "Put the safety back on your weapon, pull your hand out very slowly, and lay your weapon on the table." When the man hesitated, Luke dug his weapon in a little harder. "You're not going anywhere, so you might as well do what we say."

"We're leaving with this woman!" The man refused to move.

Murphy slid from the booth and yanked the man out, his hand reaching for the weapon. "It's like this, pal. Your friend out there in that car is already surrounded by law enforcement, and they're heading this way to take you in." He shoved the man ahead of him towards the door.

Luke holstered his weapon and then slid down by Abigail, reaching to draw her into a hug. "Are you okay?" He felt her nod, then spoke again, "We'll get out of here now. The officers have the two. But we'll have to go in and give a statement."

Abigail nodded again. "He's one of the two, Luke."

Luke's hand stilled from where he was rubbing her back. "You're sure? All right, then I guess we need to speak with Frankie."

She sighed. "I guess I have to, don't I? Would today have been prevented if we had been able to see Caleb last week?"

Luke thought about that for a minute. "I don't know, Abi. It might have, but it might not have."

She sighed, then looked around him as Murphy stopped by the table.

"Ready to go, Abigail?"

"As ready as I ever will be. And can we drop the Abigail, please? Friends call me Abi. Abigail sounds like my mother when she's telling me off."

Shocked, Murphy looked over at Luke and caught the laugh he was trying to hide. "Abi it is then. Do you want to inform the others or shall I?"

She shook her finger at him. "Behave yourself, Murphy, or I'll have to have a talk with your lady."

Murphy stopped in his tracks, a thought crossing his mind. "Now, that's a plan. How be our ladies come out to see you in the next day or so, or as many as can get there?"

She looked up, pleased. "I would like that. Nothing against you guys, you're good company, but sometimes a gal needs to speak with a gal."

Choking back his laughter, Luke caught her hand and headed for Joseph's truck. He wanted to keep it as light as possible for her, knowing she would face a heavy burden at the department. He also knew he would be in for a session with Abe. Would they ever be able to bring her out from the compound again? They had thought with three of them with her, that would be enough.

Caleb looked around from the white board he had been studying as he heard his name called. He didn't like the look on Eddie's face.

"I don't like that look, Eddie."

"You'll like what I have to tell you even less. Abigail was in Mac's with three of Abe's men after her follow up with the doctor. When she was left with just Murphy, the men tried to nab her. Thankfully, Joseph and Luke were there and prevented it. It was too close."

Caleb's keen eyes searched the area behind Eddie. "Where are they now?"

"Murphy and Joseph are giving their statements. I stashed Abigail and Luke in your office for now." Eddie paused, not sure how to continued. "Abigail recognized the voice of the man today as one of the men from the courthouse."

Caleb stopped in his walk to his office. "She did? Tell me we have a name?"

"We have a name, but it's not bringing up anything. We're running fingerprints now."

Caleb stopped at his office door. Please, Lord, let this be over soon. I don't think the fellows can take much more. I know my teams can't. Is this where trust comes in, Lord?

Caleb opened the door to his office and stopped. Abigail had stretched out on his couch, Luke's jacket as a pillow. Luke had found the blanket he had stashed on the bookshelf and covered her.

"How is she, Luke?" Caleb kept his voice low.

"She's hurting, Caleb in more ways than one. Today took a lot from her." Luke turned to watch Abigail. "I'm not sure how much more she can take."

"Not a lot, I would suspect. She's healing okay?"

Luke nodded. "She is. It's going to take a while yet before she's back to 100%, but the doctor is optimistic that will happen." He turned to stare at his friend. "Tell me you have news for us."

"I should shortly. Let her sleep until then." Caleb sat down in his chair and watched as Luke sank into one where he could keep his eyes on Abigail. "Have you talked to Abe about today?"

Luke shook his head. "Murphy did." Luke's eyes turned to Caleb. "He could have been shot in that booth, Caleb, and Abi gone before we could do anything, if Joseph hadn't seen something odd out the window."

"That was God's leading today, Luke. We have to go forward with this, putting our trust in His care and protection." Caleb turned to the door as he heard a tap and saw Frankie standing there. "What do you have, Frankie?"

Frankie handed him the report he had been reading. "It's what we thought. Those two are connected to her cousin. We're still working through the complete connection, but they are definitely muscle hired by him, and it looks as if they're involved in illegal arms shipments. We've been trying to catch these guys for months."

"What about known connections, contacts, friends?"

Frankie nodded. "We're working on that. Wilson has sunk his teeth into that part and I don't think he'll let go until he solves it." Frankie's eyes turn to where Abigail lay. "How is she, Luke?"

Luke shrugged. "She's coping but not as well as she would like us to think. Today scared her and I don't like that."

Luke's forceful words caught the two other men by surprise. Then, Caleb nodded. He had seen it before. And in five of Luke's team mates.

"Do you need to talk to her, Caleb?" Luke's question cut through his thoughts.

"If she's given her statement, then no, not right now. You can take her home. Joseph and Murphy are done, Frankie?"

Frankie nodded. "Joseph's gone to get his truck. Murphy's waiting for you two."

Luke crouched down by the couch. "Abi. Come on, sweetheart. Time to rise and shine."

"Go away, Luke. I'm not moving from here."

Luke grinned. "Sorry, sweetheart. Caleb wants his office back. Let's get you back to Rebel's and then you can sleep." When she didn't move, he gently gathered her up and carried her through the department, compassionate eyes following their path. Luke didn't really care, though. He just wanted to get his friend back to where he hoped she would be safe.

Chapter 14

To say Jordan Gilmore was furious would be an understatement. He had had two of his best men arrested trying to nab his cousin. The empire his father had created and he had inherited was crumbling around him, and as far as he was concerned, there was only one person responsible. Abigail. He needed to get to her. He was sure she had information he needed to continue to import his goods, but he just couldn't get through those guys around her.

He turned as his mother approached. "How did they fail, Jordan?" she asked. "It seemed so simple, just to walk up to her in a public place and walk off with her."

He gave a brisk nod. "I know. It should have been. We need to get her away from those guys. Are you sure she has the information we need?"

"Fairly sure. It has to have been in one of those court cases she transcribed. The program I installed hasn't picked out anything yet."

"If it's still running, that is. You can bet that they've found it."

She sighed. "I would guess they would have. Knowing your cousin, she would have noticed something along the way." She walked over to the window and stared out at the trees surrounding the cabin they had fled to. "Does anyone know about this place?"

Jordan shrugged. "Not that I know of. It's not connected to either one of us, but I guess if they do enough digging, they might find it. We'll need to come up with an alternative place."

She turned. "How did this happen, Jordan? We've managed for years to keep quiet and keep our business going."

"I know, Mom, I know. I don't know what happened. I'm not even sure any more that it is Abigail who ratted us out."

She stared at him. "You're not sure, and yet you're sending men after her? Which is it? Is she the one or not?"

"It has to be her. She's the only one we know who might figure it out. She was in and out of the store all the time growing up. If she saw something, she would have asked."

"Not necessarily. She can keep quiet when she wants to." His mother sighed. "So

I guess we really do need to get her. We can't call her, that's for sure." She tapped her lips as she thought. "Maybe if I call her mother and work through her."

"Don't. You can bet they'll be watching and tracking their phones."

"Then how do we get her? Those men have her in such tight custody we can't get near her."

Jordan waved a dismissal at his mother. "I'm working on something. It's going to take a day or so, but we should be able to get her by then."

She glared at her son. "Will it work any better than what you've already tried?" With that, she stormed from the room. Really, she thought. He was better trained than that. What went wrong?

Seeing Abigail perched on the couch, with no one around her, Ian walked over and dropped down beside her.

"What's up, Abi?"

She turned her head to look at him. "I don't know, Ian. I just wish this was all over and I could go back to my normal life. Not that it will ever be normal again."

"A new normal, for sure." He studied her face, seeing the dark circles under her eyes. "What can I do to help you right now?"

She shrugged. "I really don't know. There's not much I can do, with my dominant hand like this." She waved her cast and then grimaced. "See, I can't even move my hand without pain."

Ian watched her for a bit. "So what can we do? I know you're bored with reading, with doing nothing." Then he reached for her hand and pulled her to her feet. "Come on. I'm on dinner duty tonight and I could use some help."

"Yeah, right. Like I can really help?"

Ian nodded. "Of course you can. I didn't think you'd back down from a challenge."

She shook her head at him. "You must have been talking with Luke. That's his phrase."

Ian laughed. "No, but I can see that you wouldn't. So, are you up for it? I have some stuff I want to make and I could sure use your help."

"As long as it's not pity driving you, Ian."

"No way! You don't deserve pity."

Luke tracked her down later that afternoon, busy in the kitchen with Ian. He shook his head at the sight of her. "Put you to work, did he, Abi?"

She turned, a smile on her face. "He did, Luke. It's good to be useful."

Luke stopped in his tracks as he made his way across the kitchen. "I wish I had known you felt like that, Abi. I'm sure we could have come up with something earlier for you to do."

"Until the doctor gave me clearance, I couldn't do much. Now I can." She turned to Ian. "Now what do we have to do?"

"Nothing until it cooks." He turned to her with a smile. "And I thank you for your help."

Luke stood behind her, his hands on her shoulders. "I was coming to find you, Abi. Abe needs to talk with us."

"I hope it's not more restrictions, buddy. I'm ready to break out of this joint." She turned and walked away from him and out the door, Luke staring after her, mouth open.

Ian began laughing. "I think you just got told, Luke."

Luke shook his head, a wry smile on his face. "It's not the first time and not likely the last, but that's exactly what I'm afraid she'll do."

Abe looked up as Abigail knocked, then peeked in the door. "Come on in, Abi. Luke found you, did he?"

She nodded, then shot a glance behind her. "How can you keep Luke away from me, Abe? I don't want him hurt. I'm afraid for him."

Abe nodded to himself. They all were right. Abigail did care for Luke. "I don't know that we can, Abi. He's part of our security team and is assigned to your protection."

She sighed as she sat down. "That's about what I figured you said. Luke said you wanted to talk to me."

"I do, about something. We've had some new information come in, part from those two men from the other day." He hesitated before he continued. "The word on the street is that there's still a contract out on you. What exactly is involved in that, Caleb's people haven't been able to determine. It's more, I think, along the lines of we need her and her knowledge rather than get rid of her."

"Well, that's refreshing. At least they don't want to kill me yet." Abigail sat back, eyes on Abe. "So what do we do? Put me out there as a carrot before a donkey?"

Abe started laughing at her imagery and then shook his head, sobering. "No, Abi, that's exactly what we don't want to do. Caleb's been in touch with the police department in your home town and they taking precautions with your family. They may try to get to you through them."

"I figured they would. Now, again, Abe, what steps do we take?"

Abe sat back in his chair and thought, barely noticing Luke step into the office and sit beside Abigail. He knew where one was the other would be if possible. "We're working on that, Abi. The two men caught the other day do work for your cousin. That's been confirmed. They're not low level employees either."

She studied her hands, her thoughts tracing back over her life and how it entwined with her cousin. "They have a couple of cabins and another home, you know. They're not under their names or the company name."

"How do you know that?"

She shrugged. "Aunt Mel sometimes talked when she shouldn't have or left paperwork around where anyone could see it." She raised her eyes to Abe. "I wasn't snooping, but I noticed the general area where they were located and the names. It just struck me as odd that the places wouldn't be in their own names."

Abe reached to hand her a tablet and a pen, then stopped. "I guess you're not able to write them out. Where are they?"

Abigail recited the locations she could remember and the names the places were listed under. "I think there are likely more, either close to here or our home area. I can remember William talking about investing in property but I don't remember much talk of it after he died, almost as if he hadn't."

Abe looked up at her. "This is a good start, Abi. Now what do we do with you?"

She shrugged. "I have no idea, but if something doesn't change soon, I'm out of here." She stood and walked away, leaving the two men staring after her.

"She really mean that, Luke?"

Luke nodded. "She never has been one to sit around, and this has really tested her. I found her in the kitchen with Ian, helping him cook dinner."

Abe shook his head. "I guess we'll have to find something…" His voice broke off as he looked at his phone. "This isn't good, Luke. They were transferring the two men to Oak City, and they've escaped. The two officers with them are in hospital."

Luke sat forward in his chair. "Then I guess that means they'll be coming back after Abi." He stood and started pacing. "I just wish it hadn't been her, Abe. Now what?"

"Now what means I get to go talk with Caleb and see what he plans. Maybe we can get her away somewhere from here for a bit. Ian could fly her out." Abe paused. "Let me think on that and talk to Caleb, see what we can come up with. In the meantime, can you talk to her and let her know what's gone down?"

Luke nodded. "She won't like it. She's ready for it to end today."

Chapter 15

Caleb looked up from his paperwork as Eddie stopped in his office doorway and then sighed. He knew that look.

"What's happened that I don't want to know about, Eddie?"

Eddie stood and stared at Caleb. "Those two men we were sending to Oak City? They're on the lam and the two Oak City officers are in hospital. Frankie and Wilson were headed out there to find out what actually happened."

Caleb dropped his pen to his desk and sat back. "So, now they're loose again? And here's Abe."

"I'm getting tired of this, Caleb. How do I keep her safe?" Abe was angry and his uncle knew it took a lot to get him there. "Where do I put her now? And here. Here's a list of property locations and names Abi's come up with connected to the cousin's family."

"She's just now giving it to you?"

"Don't start with me, Caleb. I'm at my limit now. I've given that information to Tracker's as well." Abe turned and walked away, anger in his bearing. The two officers exchanged a glance, then Caleb handed Eddie the paper.

"Give it to our team, Eddie and see what they come up with."

Micah approached Abigail that afternoon. "Abi, can I talk to you for a minute?"

She turned, eyes mutinous. "If it's to tell me I'm still a prisoner, then no."

"Has it been that bad?" Micah's eyes studied her. "No, it's something we need to do. Chances are they'll make a try for you again. We just need to be sure that we can find you." He held up two minuscule objects. "I've been brainstorming with Abe and come up with these."

"What are those?"

"One's a tracking device. The other is a listening device. Trust me. Neither will activate unless you do it. I'll show you how."

"So where do these go?" Abigail leaned closer to study them.

"We tuck them into the edge of your cast, at the top edge. I've made them in such a way that you won't feel them. I talked to John Thompson. He says there shouldn't be a problem with you wearing them. We just put a little tear in the fabric, and tuck them in there. We can pull them out if we need to, say for when you go back for your checkup in two weeks, if we're still as we are."

"Lovely thought, that." She studied Micah's face and saw the concern and determination there to keep her safe. "Okay, let's get them set."

Micah folded back the sleeve of the T-shirt she was wearing and then carefully tucked the two devices into the top of her cast. "This should work. No one will know they are there, even if they are tracking something. I've worked a little magic that way. There's a little catch on each one that keeps them in place. I'll be able to get them out for you." Then he handed her a bracelet. "This is what you will use to turn them on and off. See this green stone here? If you press it once, it turns on the devices. Press the blue stone and it turns them off. Just be careful, though, that you don't play with it or you may end up turning it off and on all the time."

"That wouldn't be good, now would it?" She laughed at the look on his face. "Don't worry, Micah. I almost never wear jewelry and when I do, I don't touch it until I take it off." She studied the bracelet, and then asked, "Will this really work?"

"I pray it does, Abi, and that way we know where you are if something happens." He studied her cast, and then looked at her. "If you're not comfortable with the bracelet I can see if I can work something else out."

She shook her head. "Let's see how this works." She went to continue when her phone rang She reached for it, then went still.

"What it is, Abi?" Micah knew something was odd about the call.

"It's my aunt. I'm going to let it go to voice mail, and see what she says. I would rather not talk to her." She waited until she saw the voice mail icon light up. With Micah close to her phone, she called her voice mail and listened.

"She didn't leave a message. That's strange, Micah."

"Not if she wanted to speak with you and she knew it would go to voice mail after a certain number of rings. Is that her normal number?"

Abigail nodded. "Can Caleb trace where it came from, do you think?

"I can. Come on, let's head out to the office." Micah grabbed for her hand and pulled her with him. "I have as much or more equipment for searching that Caleb's people do and I have the time right now that they don't have."

Abigail sat and watched as Micah's fingers flew over the keyboard once again and he brought up program after program. Then he stopped.

"We have her. She's in town, would you believe it?" He reached for his phone, then hesitated. "I need to call this in, Abi. They are looking for her."

Abigail nodded. "I know. Go ahead. Maybe if they can find her, it will be all over." She rose from her chair and paced the office, her mind tuning out what Micah was saying.

Micah pocketed his phone and watched as Abigail paced. Lord, his prayer went, please help her to trust You no matter what happens. Murphy would say You have a plan and a purpose. I guess you do, but Luke's lady is hurting right now.

Luke peeked into the office, then entered when he found Abigail there. Frowning, he watched her pacing, then turned to Micah.

"Micah, what's up?"

Micah turned his eyes from watching Abigail. "Her aunt called her a while ago. I tracked her to being in town. I've given the police her approximate location. I'm just waiting to hear back if they find her." He nodded at Abigail. "Those devices we talked about? Abi's wearing them now. They tucked down nicely inside her cast. We can pull them out without an issue. We just have to watch her bracelet, that she doesn't set it off at the wrong time."

"Is there no other way to have it other than a bracelet?" Luke was worried about her losing the bracelet.

Micah nodded. "I could have done earrings but she doesn't wear any. Does she usually wear a watch?"

Luke nodded. "She used to on her right wrist. Would that work instead?"

Micah shrugged. "It might but the bracelet made more sense. She would be more apt to touch the bracelet than a watch."

Luke nodded. "I get you." He stopped as Micah's phone rang and Abigail spun around to watch him.

"That's great, Eddie. I'll let her know. Keep us in the loop with what's happening." Micah slowly pocketed his phone, his eyes on

Abigail. "Abi, they've arrested your aunt. She was at her home."

"She came back to her own house? Why? Was she so arrogant that she figured she'd never get caught?"

Micah shrugged. "They'll keep her in jail for now. Caleb said they're working through the charges, but attempted murder is likely to be there or else conspiracy to commit murder. That will put her bail really high. He's hoping he can track down the rest of the group and arrest them before she makes bail."

Luke studied the face of his friend and saw the sorrow there. "I'm sorry, Abi. I know it hurts." He walked over and drew her into a hug.

She nodded, her hair brushing his chin. "Who tells Mom and Dad about this?"

"Eddie or Frankie were going to call them, Caleb said." Micah watched the two, a puzzled look on his face. "Which side of the family is she on, Abi?"

She raised her head and looked at him, trying to determine why he was asking. "My Dad's side. Why?"

"Did they have any other siblings?"

She shrugged. "Dad always talked about a brother, but he left home as soon as he could and Dad lost track of him." She stopped speaking, a look of disbelief and horror on her face. "You don't think he's involved, do you?"

Micah shrugged. "We'll need to track him down. Let me have his name and birthdate if you know it and I'll pass it on."

She looked at Micah, then up at Luke. "Luke, when will it stop?"

Luke stared down at his childhood friend, wanting to make it all better for her, but knowing he couldn't. He knew he loved this lady and prayed she returned his love. How did he protect her though, when they didn't know who all was involved or when they would strike next?

Micah looked up from his computer and caught the look on Luke's face. Another one, Lord. Help us to keep her safe for him. "I just spoke with Eddie, Abi. He's going to get the team working on it. I'm also going to speak with Jace at Tracker's and see if he has time to run this for us."

She nodded, a distant look on her face. The two men exchanged a glance. What was she thinking and what would she try?

"Abi?" Luke's voice finally got her attention.

"What, Luke?" She turned to stare at him, giving nothing away in her look.

"I know that face. What are you plotting?"

"Nothing, at the moment. Just thinking of what I could do, that I won't be allowed to do." She turned and walked away from them and out of the office.

"Is she plotting something, Luke?" Micah's quiet question made him stop in his tracks.

"I would say she is, but I really don't know any more. She's changed." Luke hesitated as if to say more, then walked away after Abigail.

Chapter 16

Jordan turned from the two men standing in front of him. That they had been able to get to them and get them away from the authorities was a miracle, or what he classed as a miracle. It didn't bother him that men had been hurt in the escape. They were incidental to him. He looked over at his second-in-command, and stopped.

"What are you not telling me?" His voice was harsh.

"Your mother went back to town and apparently tried to call your cousin. She's been arrested."

Jordan looked at the glass in his hand and then threw it at the wall, curses flying from his mouth. "She did what? Was she stupid or something? You can bet they won't let her out of jail now."

He paced, his agitation growing with each step. His very livelihood and lifestyle were at stake, and he laid the blame directly on his cousin. He needed to find her and seek his retaliation against her.

"Leave me," he ordered the men. "I need to think and plan."

Jordan paced his office, plans running through his head and then discarded. How could he get to her? That place they had her was too tight to get into too, security-wise. Then, he stopped. He knew how to get her and he would start putting in place his plans. They would not fail this time.

He barked a come in at a knock at the door and then stopped, holding himself rigid. His uncle stood there, his uncle Ted who no one had seen in years. Sudden fear ran through him. What did he want?

"Jordan." Ted Gilmore stood and watched his nephew. "I hear you are having problems."

"I don't need your help." Jordan was defiant. "I have a plan."

"You do, do you? Will it work any better than what you have already tried?"

Jordan stared at him, then turning his back, ordered him from his house. Ted stood for a moment, then shaking his head, walked away. Jordan had a lot to learn, Ted thought. He's not fit to run the organization his father left him. Ted had been a silent figurehead in the past, but time had come for him to step up to the plate and take over.

Luke looked around for Abigail. He thought she was somewhere in the yard. Not seeing her, he headed for the house.

"Have you seen Abi?" he asked as he passed Nathaniel.

Nathaniel shook his head. "No, but Matt was looking for her a while ago. He had something for her. I think they were heading for the lake."

Luke nodded his thanks, then turned to head back out when he heard Abe's voice.

"Luke, where's Abi?"

"That's what I was trying to do, find her. Nathaniel said Matt was looking for her and they were heading for the lake."

"The lake?" Abe stopped, then hit the door of the house on a run. "Come on. Let's hope we're in time. Eddie just got word her cousin's in our area and headed for the lake. He seems to think he can snatch her from there."

They slid to a stop as they approached the lake. There was no sign of the two.

"Luke, head back and make sure they're not anywhere around the buildings. Some of the team are still around today. Find them. I just hope we're not too late." Abe stopped. "Find Micah. Get him to check her tracking device and see if she's activated it. It may be the only hope we have to find her if she's missing."

Luke shot Abe a searching look and then turned to run for the buildings. Nathaniel spun in a circle studying the area.

"How sure is Eddie that her cousin would try a grab here?"

"He got word from an undercover officer working in the group. Apparently, Jordan's come up with this idea. The other thing too, their uncle is back, and it sounds as if he's taking over the organization."

"Lovely, just what we need." Nathaniel pointed to the right. "I'll head that way if you go the other." He stopped. "I wish we had our radios."

"We don't have time now to go and get them. We'll use our phones." Abe paused as he heard his name called. Micah was running his way.

"She's activated the devices, Abe. They must have nabbed her." He thrust their com links at the two men. "We're behind the game. I'm heading back to track her."

"Let me know what you find." Abe turned and strode rapidly away, eyes moving and searching the area. Lord, how did they do this? How did they get past Matt? And where is he?

"Where's Matt?" Nathaniel's question over the link echoed Abe's.

"I hope they're together, Nathaniel. Pray they are."

Abigail shrugged the hand from her shoulder. She wanted no contact with that man, that beast, she termed him, who worked for her cousin. How did they manage to get in and get them? She reached for her bracelet, and with a quick look, pressed the stone Micah had told her to push. She prayed that this would work, that they would be able to track them. If not, then who knew how they would be found. She stumbled as she climbed the rock trail. Matt, walking beside her, reached for her hand. A strong blow to his arm left it feeling numb and useless. Abigail shot a glance behind her, then catching Matt's eye, pointed at her bracelet. A nod from him let her know he was aware she had turned on the tracking device.

Roughly shoved into a luxury sedan, the trail led away from the compound. Abigail was scared, more scared than she could ever remember being. She had been told her cousin wanted to see her. She snorted to herself. Yeah, right, like that's the truth. He only wants something from me.

Matt sat beside Abigail, mind racing. How could he get them out of this mess? And did the team even know yet that they were missing? He hoped they did and that the tracking device was working. Right now, that seemed to be their only chance. He studied the men in the front seat and sitting beside Abigail. Too many, he thought, for me to take out on my own. Lord, if You have a plan, now would be a really great time to tell me.

Matt's eyes narrowed as he watched the man in the front passenger seat. Something was off about him. He didn't quite fit the character of the other two men. The man gave him a quick glance and then a faint shake of the head. Interesting, Matt thought. I wonder what side he's really on.

Abigail slumped back in the seat, shoulder leaning on Matt. She wanted out of that car, but didn't know how she could escape. She certainly didn't want to confront her cousin. He had a cruel streak, one that she had felt in the past, and she figured it had only gotten worse. How did he fool them into letting him become a judge, she wondered? Or better yet, who did he pay off?

The car slowed for a turn, and that's when the front passenger acted. He slammed his fist into the driver's face. Before the man in the back could react, Matt had Abigail down on the floor and his fist was flying at the man beside her. The front seat passenger steered the car to the side of the road and pulled on the emergency brake.

He turned to Matt and Abigail. "We need to get out of here. They'll be looking for us."

"Who are you?" Abigail refused to leave the seat.

Matt pulled her out his door. "It doesn't matter right now, Abi. We need to disappear and I think our friend will be with us."

The man nodded. "I have to now. I think I just blew my cover. But I couldn't let them take you to the house. Abi would have disappeared and never been seen in this country again. You, they would have just dumped your body somewhere." He reached for the glove compartment and pulled out handcuffs, handing one set to Matt. "Let's cuff them, dump them, and then take off. I think we have enough time we can get away. I just hope your team isn't right behind us."

"They'll be tracking us, I imagine." Matt stood upright from handcuffing the man, then looked around. "I think you'll find they have a tracking device on this vehicle. I suggest we leave it. I know the area around here. Let's head that way." He pointed to the right. "It takes us towards where we were going, but then we can split off from there and find shelter for the night." He looked down at Abigail. "Are you up to this, Abi?"

She nodded. "I have no choice. There is no way I'm going anywhere near my cousin."

"Your uncle's here too. He's taking over the business from your cousin." The man looked around. "Look, I know you don't know me or even trust me. Believe me when I say they had plans for you. My name's Shane. The last name isn't important. If I don't check in by tomorrow, my contact on the outside will be looking for me. That could get me killed." Shane looked around. "We can't use their phones and they took mine from me."

"Mine was taken and thrown somewhere." Matt lead the way, Abigail close on his heels.

Two hours later, Matt brought them to a halt. Abigail gratefully sank to the ground, tired beyond what she had ever been.

"How much further, Matt?"

He turned to her from watching the area around him. "Not far, Abi. We need to catch our breath and see if we're being followed. If we are, then I'll have to head in another direction."

Shane nodded. "I'll check out our back trail. I've done some hiking in the area as well."

They listened to him move way. Then Abi spoke in a low voice. "Micah, if this is really working and you can hear me, we're free of the men, but there's someone with us. Matt's taking us up the hill and then over. Please, hurry."

Abe's com link clicked as he reached for the phone he had found. Matt's, he thought.

"Abe, Abi's just got word to me that they're free of the men but there's someone with them. I'll try and see if they can get a full name for me. From what I've heard, he's been undercover."

"Just what we need. How do we know we can trust him?" Abe's voice was tight with worry and frustration.

"We don't. I guess that where our trust comes in."

Abe turned as he heard footsteps approaching. Luke and Nathaniel were there.

"Where to now, Abe?" Luke was worried and had a hard time covering up that fact.

"We'll find them, Luke. Matt's walking them out. I just don't like that there's someone else with them."

Nathaniel shook his head. "I don't either. Micah's been in touch with Caleb, and he's working the angle, trying to determine who it might be. I don't like the fact that he's saying her uncle's around."

"I don't either." Luke thought about the man he had heard about. "I understand he has a real sadistic streak."

Abe nodded. "From what that Shane said, he was planning on taking Abi out of the country. Who knows what his plans for her would have been. We need to get to them and get them to safety." Abe looked around, not seeing anything else. "Caleb's sent a team out to search up where Joseph found evidence of a car. Let's head back and then out for the area where we know they're heading. That is, if we can do that without anyone tracking us."

Luke nodded. "That's the problem. We don't know if they've left anyone around to follow us, or a worse thought, that while we've been off site, they've managed to get in and place trackers on the vehicles."

Abe stopped walking and turned and stared at Luke. "I would suspect they have. That's why we're not taking our vehicles. I've made arrangements for Doug and his ETF to meet us in town. They'll be with us when we go in to get our two out."

Chapter 17

Doug Foster, ETF lieutenant, watched as Abe and his team pulled in beside him. His eyes searched the area around them, but couldn't see that they had had a tail.

Abe walked over to where Doug was standing. "Are we set, Doug?"

Doug watched his cousin, seeing the strain of the last few hours in his face. "We are. It'll be a little crowded, but we should be fine. Does Micah have his laptop that we can hook into ours for the tracking devices?"

Abe nodded. "He's been tracking them with his phone for now. He'll give you the coordinates so we can get underway." Abe stopped. "Thanks for stepping up for us."

Doug shrugged. "We watch each other's backs, Abe. We always have, you and I. Our teams are the same. Let's get you loaded and on the way." He stopped for a minute. "Just what does Micah have going on?"

Abe gave a short laugh. "He rigged up a tracking device and a voice transmitter small enough he could tuck them into Abi's cast and then set up a bracelet that she could use to turn them on and off. Smart lady was able to get them working. That's how we know where they are." He stopped for a minute, lost in thought. "Only thing is, they've picked up someone who says he's been working undercover."

"Did you pass on his name to Eddie or Frankie?" Doug's eyes were keen and didn't miss the emotions flickering across any of the team's faces.

"I did, but he only gave a first name. I can tell neither of them trust him too far. It would be easy to fake this and then lead them right into her cousin's arms."

Luke sat back, watching the commotion going on around him, his eyes fixed on Micah and the ETF computer expert. He prayed they would find them soon, like before dark, please Lord. Then he stopped. He couldn't dictate to God what happened. Murphy would tell him to trust, that God was in control.

Abigail looked around Matt as she heard soft footsteps, her breath catching in her throat. Matt turned towards the noise as well, only relaxing a little as he saw Shane step back into view.

"So far, so good." Shane studied the two in front of him, knowing they didn't trust him, but he didn't know how to get them to. His proper identification was hidden in a post office box in Riverville. He prayed that they would trust him as he needed to get them moving. They had a follower, and he hoped it wasn't who he thought it was. If it was, they had to really move to get ahead of him.

"Anyone behind us?" Matt's eyes went past Shane, then back to him.

"There is. I just hope it isn't who I think it is. If it is, we're in trouble. He's good. He works for Jordan's uncle and is like a terrier on a trail."

Abigail shook her head. "I just want this over, Matt. What do I know what they want from me?"

Matt shook his head as he helped her to her feet. "I don't know, Abi. There has to be something. They wouldn't be that determined to get to you if there wasn't something."

Shane watched them as they moved off in front of him and then made a decision. "I can tell you what it is. They think your friend here has information as to the site of a large pile of armaments that haven't been found yet. They think she's come across that in some of her work."

Abigail stopped and stared back at him. "There is no way that kind of information was in any of the trials that I transcribed. If it wasn't in the transcripts of the trial, then I don't know where this pile of stuff is." She turned and marched off, the two men exchanging a glance, then following.

"Abi, wait, let one of us go ahead of you, please." Matt waited for her to respond. When she didn't, he called her again in an angry voice. "Abigail. Stop right now."

She stopped, then sighed. "I'm sorry, Matt. I did what Abe asked me not to do."

Micah shook his head as he listened to the conversation through his headset. "Abe, they're after a pile of armaments that they think Abi knows the location for. Can you pass that on to Eddie or Frankie?"

Abe nodded, reaching for his phone. "Now, it's beginning to make sense. But with her cousin being a judge, doesn't he get it that kind of information is never in the transcripts unless it's in the trial?"

Doug spoke up. "From what I'm beginning to understand about her cousin, I don't think he really cares. If he can use her to trade for the armaments, then he will." He shot a look at Luke, sitting there, taking it all in. "Luke, how much would she tell them?"

"Nothing, if she doesn't know what they want. Otherwise, she would come up with a plausible place for them to look. That's what I'm afraid she'll try if they get ahold of them again."

Micah spoke up. "They're on the move again. The fellow with them, Shane, back tracked and they've picked up a trail. Let's pray that we can get to them first."

Matt stopped for a minute, to let them catch their breath. "Shane, how did you get mixed up in this?"

Shane shot him a look from where he leaned against a tree. "If you're asking what branch of law enforcement, I'd rather not say. That's to protect you. If you're asking my last name, it's Taylor." He looked behind him. "We need to keep moving. Is there a cabin or a road over the top of the hill, Matt?"

"There're a number of trails we can take, they branch off from one another. There should be enough deadfall we can set some traps as well. They didn't do a very thorough search." He pulled back his pant leg and showed them a knife he had hidden there.

"Good. I have my weapon but that's not going to help us get away." He turned to Abigail. "Now, we need to figure out how to get you out of here."

Abigail shook her head. "We'll get there. It's just a matter of staying ahead of them." She shifted the sling she was wearing. Matt eyed it and then lifted his eyes to hers and nodded. Everything was still going through, he hoped, and he hoped that Micah was still reading the signals.

"Abe, we have a last name for Shane. It's Taylor. He's not saying who he's working for."

"I'm on it, Micah." Abe spoke with Eddie, then watched as the large van slowed and turned into the wooded area. "What side of the hill are they on, Micah?"

"The opposite side, and I can hear Matt coming up with a plan. There's a hitch though. He's saying rain's moving in and they're going to have to go to ground somewhere."

"Not what I want to hear." Abe turned to Doug. "Your show, Doug. Your call."

"How close are we to them, Micah?"

Micah conferred with the computer tech, then looked around. "Twenty miles or so by road. About a quarter of that if we head inland."

Doug stared at Abe, silent communication going between the two men. These two men had worked together for years, had played together and fought with one another as youngsters, but had each other's back when it mattered. "How well prepared are your guys to move out in the rain, Abe?"

"We're ready." Nathaniel spoke up from where he had been standing, leaning against the wall of the van. "We have our rain gear with us."

Abe nodded. "We're good to go if that's what you decide, Doug."

Doug nodded, then leaned forward to speak with the driver. The van pulled over and stopped. Doug turned to Abe. "Okay, we'll split up. We need Micah to stay with us, though."

Abe nodded. "Thought you would. We're linked into his computer and he can talk with us." He looked around at the five team members he would have with him. "Before we head out, guys, let pray."

Abe led the way up the trail, praying they would reach the three in time. He could heard the soft footsteps behind him.

Abigail stopped walking. She just needed to catch her breath. She didn't think she was that out of shape, but climbing this hill proved otherwise.

"Are you okay?" Matt walked back to stand beside her, eyes roaming the area. Shane stood, eyes watching their back trail.

"I am, Matt. I just needed to catch my breath." She lowered her voice so only Matt could hear her. "Do you think this is working, that Micah's able to track us?"

"If he said it would work, then yeah it is." Matt studied her, then looked over at Shane. "He'll be able to pass on information to Abe." Raising his voice again, he motioned to her to come. "Come on, Abi. We need to keep moving. I want to find somewhere to hole up. Rain's getting closer."

She sighed. "You just had to mention that, didn't you?"

Matt grinned at her. "See, you're grumbling."

"And that was your whole purpose of this, right?" Her disgruntled voice followed him down the trail. They had crested the hill and were working their way down to the other side.

A yell from Shane stopped them in their tracks and they looked backwards. Then, Matt grabbed for Abigail's hand.

"They've found us, Abi. We need to get you hidden."

Gasping for breath as she ran, encumbered by her sling and cast, she glanced behind her.

"Matt, where are you going?"

"Shh. In here." He parted some branches and pushed her inside a thicket. "Stay down. We'll have some protection from the rain. Let's pray they think we're still running."

Heart pounding, Abigail lay on the damp ground, head buried in her arm. Mat crouched beside her, head turning and eyes watchful. Where were they? He hadn't heard anything from Shane since that yell.

"They have to be along here somewhere." A rough voice broke into the stillness. "Find them."

Matt heard Abigail give a gasp, and he turned to study her.

"That voice sounds familiar, Matt. Who is it?" Her voice was low enough that Matt barely heard her.

His eyes turned once more to the front of the thicket, he waited. Then a small whisper of sound came and he was down before he could turn. He heard the sound of Abigail's scream, then nothing.

Rough hands grabbed Abigail and dragged her from the thicket, Matt dragged out behind her and dropped heavily to the ground. She stared at the man standing in front of her, horror coursing through her. They had been free, now were caught. If only she knew how Abe was close.

The man standing watching her eyed her in a dispassionate manner. Niece or not, she really didn't matter to him, except as a means to getting what he wanted. His eyes turned to Matt, then raised back to her.

"Where is it, Abigail?"

She trembled with fear, shaking her head. "I don't know what you want."

"The location of the armaments, my dear." He motioned to one of his men, standing near Matt, who now had aimed his weapon at Matt.

Matt struggled to his feet, eyes blurring as he watched those around him. Abigail's eyes were fastened on her uncle, head shaking as she denied knowing where the armaments were.

Micah listened to the quiet chatter coming from his own team as his attention focused on Abigail's voice. Hurry, Abe, I really don't know how long you have to get to them.

Then, sitting back, he had a look of horror on his face. The tech beside him shot him a glance and then looked back at Doug. Doug, a puzzled look on his face, moved forward and pulled the headset off Micah and then pulled the plug from the laptop. Silence filled the van as the men listened.

Then, Abigail's sobs broke through the silence and the agony in her voice caused even the most hardened of the officers to pause.

"No! No! Please! Don't hurt him any more! Please! Don't kill him! Please!" Abigail could barely get the words out for her sobs.

"Then, tell us where to find it." The cruelty in the voice came through and Micah shuddered at the thought of the two facing this monster on their own.

"Micah, how close are we?" Abe's voice broke through the darkness Micah was under. "Micah? Come on, Micah, talk to me."

"Abe, uh. Yeah. Abe, it looks like you're within a half mile of them, but they're moving away from you, back down towards the road they're on. It's a shorter path than what they just walked up."

"All of them?" Abe's voice held a question he couldn't voice.

"So far, I think so. Thev've found them. I know Matt and Abigail are with them." Micah's voice died away again as he heard Abigail once more pleading with her uncle not to hurt Matt, and his eyes slid shut in prayer. Then there was just the muted sounds of conversation and Abigail's soft sobs.

"It's not looking good, Abe. You need to get there. We're coming up around the hill, but if they have vehicles waiting, then we may not make it in time." Micah looked back at Doug, grim lines on both their faces. "I haven't heard anything from that Shane they said was with them."

"We'll watch for the him. Just keep me in the loop as to where they are."

Murphy moved up beside Abe, shooting a look back at Luke. "What's he not saying, Abe?"

Abe nodded, his eyes in constant motion, his hand pulling his com link away from his mouth. "I know. That worries me, Murphy. Pray we're in time. I don't want to have to tell Luke Abi didn't make it. Nor do I want to face Sarah about Matt."

A whisper of noise to the side had them halting, weapons raised to face whoever was there. Abe nodded and Joseph and Nathaniel moved towards the noise, confident that their team members had them covered. Nathaniel reached into the brush and pulled the man hiding there out. Face covered in blood, he stood swaying, trying to focus on the group of men in front of him.

"You must be Shane." Abe's voice held certainty.

Shane studied him as best he could, then nodded. "I am. You must be the ones looking for those two."

"We are. Where are they?"

"Ahead of you, I suspect. The uncle is adamant that she tells him where the armaments are." Shane swayed again, and Nathaniel's hand came out to hold him upright.

"We need to keep moving, but I don't know if you're able to keep up." Abe studied the man, knowing that he would do his best to keep up with them. "Stay to the back of my men. Come on, guys. Micah thinks

they're heading for vehicles, and I want to
stop that if I can."

Chapter 18

Abigail slumped in the car seat, despondent that they hadn't gotten away, terrified at being in her uncle's hands. She had never met him, but the resemblance to her own father was there, in looks only. His cruelty in no way matched her father's gentle personality. Matt's hand rested on her cast as he tried to recover from the beating he had taken. She turned her head just a bit to watch as he laid his head down on the seat back, blood on his face, and bruises and swellings forming. Why, Lord? We were so close to getting away. What happened? Help me to trust You now because on my own, I just can't. She swiped at the tears on her face, disgusted with herself that she had broken down.

Matt's head turned at the motion from Abigail, and he watched as she moved quietly. What was she planning? He could tell she was up to something. Then his eyes closed, the pain and discomfort he was feeling winning over his need to protect Abigail.

Her uncle turned slightly to watch her, an unreadable look on his face. She looks like her mother, he thought, then turned to watch the road ahead. Just where were those weapons? Jordan was useless, he decided, and he would get rid of him as soon as he could.

Abigail studied what she could of the area around them, seeking to find a way to escape. She needed to get Matt out of there, to his friends, to help. She really didn't care if she made it, she just wanted Matt safe and back with his Sarah. She wouldn't be able to live with herself if he didn't make it. Eyes turned to her uncle, she watched and listened to him planning. She knew her days were numbered, but what was this about taking her out of the country? There was no way she'd do that.

Bringing the car to a halt near an outbuilding, the driver opened the back door and motioned for Matt to exit. Matt didn't move, his brain not comprehending what was asked of him. He was hauled out of the vehicle and shoved violently towards the building, stumbling as he tried to keep his balance. Matt could hear Abigail behind him, footsteps faltering as she was also dragged to the building. Bringing them to a halt in the middle of the garage, her uncle stood and stared at them.

"I'll give you one hour, young lady, and then I'll be back. Be prepared to share the location, or your friend here is dead, and you'll be on a plane out of the country. Maybe then you'll talk." He turned and walked away, in his depravity not caring that it was his own family he was talking to.

He found one of his men and sent them after Jordan. Jordan would not be making any decisions regarding the business any more, he thought. Then, an evil smile crossed his face. He wouldn't be making decisions of any kind any more.

Abe stood, hand to the frame of the van bracing his stance, his eyes on Luke. Luke's eyes were glued to the computer, his face shuttered. Abe could usually read something there, but at this point, there was nothing there to read. Luke, we need you to be part of the team right now. I don't want to make you sit out. He turned with a quiet word to Doug.

Doug turned to Shane, studying the man they had picked up in their travels that day. Then, he nodded. He knew now who he was and who he worked for. "Shane, where are we heading?"

Shane shook off the fog he was under, and gazed over at Doug. "There's an old house up ahead, about five miles from where you picked us up. No one knows about it. It's not registered in any of their names."

Abe spoke up. "Is it registered under a numbered company?" When he gave the company number, Shane nodded.

"I don't know how you know but that's it."

"Abigail saw that name years ago and had buried it in her mind. She gave it me a day or so ago. Doug, have you been in touch with Caleb?"

"I have. He's working on warrants but I don't think we'll have time to get them to us." He looked down as his phone chimed with a text message. "He's got them, and sent me copies. Bob, print out what I've just sent you. The judge has agreed that copies will suffice if needed when we get there. Caleb's arranging for a chopper to bring the originals out with Eddie and Frankie, once we determine this is the right spot. Shane, how far away is it safe to stop?"

"About now. They usually have one or two men walking the perimeter. I don't think they've had time to bring in the dogs. Those two getting away kind of ruined their plans.

They were to have been brought to the cabin Jordan was staying at."

Doug handed over a clipboard, paper and pen. "Draw us a picture, Shane. You've been there. You're our best hope to get to them and get them out."

Shane nodded, thought for a minute, then began to draw. "Here. There's a main house, not large, 2-3 bedrooms, great room, two baths, large kitchen. All on one floor, no basement." He continued to draw. "There's a detached garage about 50 feet from the house. I suspect it was a barn at one time that was converted. Just one large room, no loft." He tapped his finger on the paper. "That's where they're likely to be. It has a dirt floor, and it's easy to hide evidence of crime. I've heard that's what her uncle has done."

The men in the van shared grim glances as the driver slowed, then stopped the van.

"What else?" Luke's harsh voice broke into the silence.

"There's woods and shrub brush up close to the back of the garage. They don't keep it trimmed back, trying to make it look as if it's not used a lot. That will work to our advantage, I think." Shane's eyes roamed to each man in the van, most of them with their eyes on him. "I know you don't know me or even if you can trust what I'm telling you. But trust me on this. If we don't get to them now, we won't get to them alive, or at the very least, Abigail will have disappeared. Her uncle has plans to send her out of the country. I've seen him do that before."

Abe and Doug shared a look. There was no way that was happening. Abe's eyes turned to each of his men and saw the same determination there.

"Okay, men. Here's the plan." Doug laid out his plan, sending his own sniper and Nathaniel, Abe's sniper, out to find a high spot they could see from.

Abe's men had been assigned to the garage, Doug's men to the house. After a quick word of prayer, all knowing they needed divine intervention if it was to work, they quietly moved out, their dark clothing melding with the growing darkness and dampness brought on by the rain and coming night.

The two teams spread out, moving in quietly on their objectives. Micah and his counterpart on Doug's team waited, knowing there would be silence until the teams reached their objectives.

Abigail paced the garage, looking for a way out. She knew the hour was drawing to a close. What could she tell them that would buy them a few more hours, a chance for Abe to reach them? She knew without a shadow of a doubt that Abe's team was following them. Micah had assured her the transmitter and tracker would work. Abe she picture as a wolf, tracking his prey, his prey being them. She turned to study Matt, slumped against the wall of the building. He was hurting, she knew, just because he happened to be the one with her earlier that day.

Caleb stood in the conference room, studying the fluctuating information on the white board, and then turned to find Eddie.

"Where do we stand, Eddie?"

Eddie looked up from the reports he was flipping through. "Frankie's on his way to the airport with the warrants, hoping they can get a chopper up in the air, given the rain. Doug's team and Abe's team are moving in on the buildings. Jace at Tracker's is feeding our lab techs information so fast they can't keep up with it, needing to verify it ourselves. He's so good, I wished he'd come work for us."

"No, he won't, but we should see about bringing Tracker's in as consultants. That way we can use their information without having to verify it." Caleb searched the room, nodding at the team that had been assembled. His best men and women officers were there. "We've got a good team here, Eddie. How's Wilson working out?"

"He's good, Caleb. Give him a year or two and a few cases, and there'll not likely be many who can beat him at digging out information. He's young, but he's eager to learn, cautious until he verifies his information, and digs until he finds what he needs to find."

Caleb nodded. "Good. We brought him in on a temporary basis on this case. I've made him a permanent part of your team. Do you want to tell him?"

Eddie looked over at Wilson and smiled. "That would give me great pleasure to do that." He turned as his name was called and a report handed to him.

"Here we go, Caleb. The uncle has a plane at Oak City airport and he's given word for it to be ready to leave within the next four hours."

Caleb had his phone out. "What's the information on the plane? I'll have the chief in Oak City step in and stop it somehow. We're not letting them get out of the country. We'd never seen them again."

Eddie nodded. "From what Micah's relaying, that's the uncle's plan for Abigail. We'd never find her."

Caleb turned and studied Eddie, not liking that thought. "I hear you. We'll keep that from happening, Eddie. I don't want to see one of Abe's men hurt that way."

Eddie shook his head, as his attention returned to the reports he held. "I don't either, Caleb. My prayer is we reach them in time."

Chapter 19

Abigail slumped down to the floor beside Matt and then tilted her head to watch him. His head back against the wall, she didn't even know if he was still awake. She was afraid, afraid that Abe's team was too far away, afraid that no one would find them in time. Lord, she prayed, please bring someone soon. My uncle will back soon and I'm not ready to face him. I'm trying to come up with a plausible place, but I just can't. She wrapped her good arm around her knees and laid her head on her knees. She was ready to give up, ready to do what she wasn't sure. She just knew help was too far away to reach them.

She didn't raise her head as the door swung open. She no longer cared whether she lived or died. Eyes locked on the floor, she didn't look up as the footsteps approached and then she was pulled to her feet and swung up in someone's arm. Her head fell onto a shoulder, and she knew no more.

Luke looked down at Abigail, then at Abe, who motioned him out the door. Joseph had Matt up and over his shoulder and out the door. Abe took a look around, and then swinging the door closed behind him, headed after his team. He knew the ambulance was waiting down the road, near the ETF van and that Doug would be advised that he had the two.

Luke laid Abigail gently on one of the stretchers, then stepped back and watched. She was just so still, he thought. What had happened to her? He turned so his eyes could trace the road down to the house and prayed that Doug's team would catch the men responsible.

Micah stood behind Luke, watching as Luke tried to determine what had gone on. He turned as Abe came up beside him.

"We'll have to tell him at some point, Abe."

"I know, Micah, but now's not the time. Let's get them help and then we can regroup as a team. This has taken a lot from all of us, but you in particular, I think."

"It has, Abe. I knew my devices would work, but I never expected to hear what we did over it. I'll never forget that."

"I don't know what all you heard, Micah, but it was bad enough I heard it in your voice. We'll talk it through." Abe turned as Doug walked towards. "Tell me you have them, Doug,"

Doug nodded. "We have the uncle and his men. Her cousin is dead, shot execution style."

The men who overheard turned and stared at Doug and then down the road to where Doug's men held the men.

Luke spun as well from where he had been standing near the ambulance. "Her uncle?"

"That's what one of the men is saying. Shane, if you had been there, it likely would have been your task to take out either the cousin or Matt. This man who shot the cousin is low man on the totem pole and was trying to prove his loyalty. His loyalty will now include murder charges." He nodded towards the ambulance. "How are they?"

Abe turned as well to watch as the ambulance door closed, Luke he noted climbing into the front seat. He shouldn't have gone, but Abe gave a nod as he looked back at him. They still needed security with them. He motioned to Joseph to head with them. "We don't know yet. We'll need an escort, Doug."

"It's already arranged. Caleb has officers on the way in as well as the crime scene team. He's heading here too."

"It's going to be a long messy night here, Doug, and I don't mean because of the rain. Trying to sort this out will take time." Abe searched the area, feeling eyes watching him again. "Somehow, I don't think we've got everyone."

Micah headed his way. "Abe, we've got a problem. I just got a text from Jace at Tracker's." He handed Abe his phone. "He's got his own family involved in the business."

Abe's heart dropped. Here, he thought they were done, and they weren't. He wasn't sure how much longer he would be able to keep Abigail in protection. She was already chafing at the restrictions. "Has Jace sent that on to Eddie or Frankie?"

Micah nodded. "He has. He's working to try and find the family, a son for sure. There were rumours of a daughter, but no one has seen her for years."

Doug and Abe shared a glance, the same thought running through their minds. "Have Jace track a passport for her and see if she's gone overseas and where."

Micah shot him a look, comprehension dawning on his face. "You don't think he would have, do you?"

Abe nodded. "I do. Go, see what you can find." He turned to Doug.

Late that night, Abe walked through the quiet hospital corridors, stopping as he came to a pair of wooden doors. He pushed them open and then sat in the last seat in the chapel. Today had taken a lot from him and a lot from his men. He needed a quiet spot for a few minutes, just to remember how good God was and to renew the trust that seemed to be on shaky grounds lately.

Eddie, on the hunt for his nephew, pushed the door open partway, then entered and slid down in the seat beside Abe. He knew Abe was hurting in more ways that one.

"Eddie, what are you doing here?" Abe's voice was muffled from where he had laid his head on his folded arms on the pew back.

"Looking for my hurting nephew." Eddie's hand went out to lay gently on Abe's back. "Talk to me, Abe. This is just more than today."

Abe nodded and turned his head so he could see his uncle. "It is, Eddie. We've been through so much lately, I don't know how much more the guys can take. Today was brutal. Micah's hurting bad." He blinked away the tears that had gathered. "He heard the beating, he heard Abi trying to stop it. Micah's heart is so tender, I don't know how to help him."

"Prayer and time, Abe. Prayer and time and your friendship. That's what it will take."

Abe nodded. "What else, Eddie?"

Eddie sighed. "Between Jace and Micah, we've been able to trace Abigail's cousin. She's dead, killed in a so-called home invasion a few years ago. The police were never satisfied that's what it was. They're reopening the case."

Abe sat back, thinking of what had been said. "It wouldn't take too much of a stretch in the imagination to figure out what happened."

Eddie shook his head, then stood. "Come. I know you're heading for Matt and Abigail's rooms. Let's get you there, then get you home to your bed."

Abe nodded, then spoke. "I'm not heading home, Eddie. I still feel like something is going to happen tonight."

"We've got guards in place, your men refuse to leave, and Luke has settled into Abigail's room, refusing to leave." He followed Abe from the chapel. "I spoke to her mom. Her parents are heading this way tomorrow. Her brother and sister can't make it tomorrow, although they'll be out later in the week. That is, if Abigail lets them. When Frankie spoke to her earlier, she was adamant she didn't want her family around her."

Abe nodded again, then stopped at Matt's door, the officer checking his identification. "I'll catch up with you tomorrow, Eddie. It's going to be a long few days or weeks I think."

"That is will be, Abe." Eddie watched as the door closed behind Abe, then studied the corridor around him. Something just didn't feel right, and he knew to go with his instincts.

Abe stood at Matt's bedside, his eyes tracing the cuts, bruises and swellings on his friend's face. What did they do, Matt? How long did they beat you?

He turned as the door opened and Matt's fiancee, Sarah, entered.

"Sarah? What are you doing here?"

She shrugged. "I can't stay away when he's hurting, Abe." She stood beside Matt's bed, then lowered the bed rail to reach for his hand. "I knew when we started dating, and after what I went through, the character of him. Now, don't start with me." She glared at Abe. "I'm not leaving."

"Didn't think you would. I was just surprised to see you here at this time of night." Abe pulled a chair up for her. "Can I get you anything?"

Sarah shook her head. "I'm good. Your team is waiting for you in the room down the hall. The hospital finally opened up a conference room for your guys."

"Thanks, Sarah. You have my number. Call if you need anything or just need to talk."

"Thank you, Abe." Her attention was on Matt, not seeing the compassion that flickered across Abe's face as he turned to leave.

Abe stood watching his team, minus Luke and Matt. They were hurting he could tell. He wasn't surprised to see the fiancees there. He expected it. He turned to walk away, when Murphy spoke beside him.

"Abe, what's up? I know that look on your face." Murphy studied his friend and partner's face.

Abe nodded towards the corridor. "Walk with me, Murphy. We need to make more plans. Eddie was in. They've found her cousin. She's dead, but the police are reopening the investigation given what happened today. The brother is still at large, and we think he'll be heading this way."

Murphy drove his hands into his pockets, frustration evident. "I guess that means Abi's back with us?"

Abe nodded. "If she'll trust us enough. I want to know how they got in there, Murphy, and if there's anything we can do to prevent it."

Murphy's eyes stared into the distance. "I'll work with Joseph and Micah and see if there's some sort of an alarm system we can put in place. We've never needed it before."

Abe agreed. "No, we haven't but this time we will." He sighed as he stopped at Abigail's door and pulled out his identification once more. "See what you three can come up with."

Abe stood just inside the closed door and slid his eyes shut for a minute. He was exhausted, just as his team once. Opening his eyes, he searched the dim room, seeing Luke slumped down in the chair near Abigail's bed, sound asleep. She must be okay if

Luke's sleeping, Lord. Heal my team and these two.

Abe walked on quiet feet to the bed and stood, watching Abigail as she moved restlessly. Her eyes opened, and she blinked, trying to focus.

"Abe? We're safe?" Her voice was hoarse but low.

"In a manner of speaking you are. How are you feeling?"

"Ok. The physician said I didn't have any new damage to the joint, which surprised them. He's releasing me in the morning." She blinked, determined not to cry. "So, now what? Where do I go?"

"Back with us, Abi." When she started to shake her head, he continued, "We have to, Abi. It's not over, not quite yet. Caleb wants you to stay with us for now, until he can get everything sorted out."

She sighed, then nodded. Turning her head, she watched Luke sleeping. "Take him home, Abe. Get him out of here. I don't want him around me."

"That's not happening, Abi. In case you missed it, he cares a great deal for you."

She shook her head again. "Take him home, Abe. He needs somewhere to sleep that's better than that chair."

Abe studied her again, then turned to walk away. "You two can argue it out."

She glared after Abe, then once more turned her eyes to Luke. He can't be comfortable there, she thought. Luke, what am I to do with you? Her eyes closed and she eased back into sleep, not hearing the nurse come in with silent feet and slip an envelope into her sling as she turned to leave again.

Abe heard the voices from Abigail's room the next morning as he approached it and shot a look at the officer, who grinned at him.

"They've been going at it for at least fifteen minutes." The officer looked behind him at the closed door. "Right now, I don't think either of them are winning."

Abe shoved the door open in frustration and the voices died away. "What's going on? I can hear you in the corridor through the closed door."

Luke glared at Abigail. "She's adamant she's not coming back to Rebel's."

"That a moot point, Luke. She is still under our protection and until we know for sure the threat is gone, that's where she'll be. If not there, then somewhere else with our whole team guarding her."

Abigail turned from the window she had been staring out. "I'm not doing it, Abe."

"You don't have a choice in the matter, Abi. If you don't come with us, Caleb has instructed the officer outside your door to arrest you and put you into custody for obstructing an investigation or at the very least, for your own safety. Take your pick." Abe had had a long conversation with Caleb that morning, and he knew it wasn't over, not by a long shot. He needed to get Abigail out of there and back to Rebel's and then work with his team once again to come up with a strategy to keep her safe, at least for a few weeks while the evidence was gathered and presented at a preliminary hearing. After that, they would see what would happen.

"Is that it, then? I'm still a prisoner?" Abigail was not happy and her words flew out to hit at the men.

"Abigail Grace Gilmore, this stops now. Everyone risked their lives yesterday to find you and bring you home. Matt's hurt because of that." Luke was furious with her, and she stopped in her walk away from them, back rigid. "Get your stuff. We're leaving now. Are you ready to go, Abe?" At Abe's nod, Luke reached for Abigail's hand. When she tried to pull way, he tightened his grip. "If you don't stop, Abi, I'll find a pair of handcuffs and handcuff you to me. Do you really want to walk out of here like that?"

Abe studied her. Something was off, he thought. Something happened last night. Excusing himself, he walked down the corridor and made a call to Eddie, telling him his suspicions. He scanned the ceiling and nodded. Security cameras, at least three he could see, were in place.

He turned as Luke and Abigail stopped beside him. He didn't like the shuttered look on her face. She was afraid, he could tell, but there was something else there. He looked up at Luke, who nodded. Luke had picked up on it too. So how did they get Abigail to talk to them?

Luke came to find Abe after settling Abigail back into the house. "What happened last night, Abe? She was fine, now this?"

Abe turned from the window he had been staring out. "Someone got to her, Luke. Somehow, someone got to her. I would think her cousin who we haven't found yet."

Luke stared at the wall ahead of him, not taking in the photos framed there. "Who and how?"

"Eddie's pulling security footage. There's a man seen at the nurses' station, handing over an envelope to Abi's nurse.

Shortly after that, the nurse is seen entering Abi's room."

"I was there, Abe."

"I know you were, Luke, but you were sound asleep. You didn't even stir when I came in to check on you. The nurses were in and out all night, so we're not sure of when the envelope was placed." Abe turned to stare towards the hallway. "We need to get it from her, and I don't think we'll have an easy time of it. It more likely contains a threat."

Abigail turned the envelope over and over in her hands, fear coursing through her. No, not fear, she thought, terror. She thought it was all over and now this. She didn't want to tell Abe. He would just tighten the security around her, putting his men at risk. After yesterday, she didn't want that. She wasn't sure who she could turn to.

A knock at the door had her hiding the envelope back into her sling. Walking across the room and opening the door, she found Luke standing there, an unreadable look on his face.

"Come on, Abi. We need to talk."

"No, we don't. There's nothing to say."

"Enough of this, Abi." Luke grabbed her hand and pulled her from the room to the living room, shoving her down on the couch. "Talk to us. What happened overnight to scare you so badly?"

"Luke, go away." Abigail refused to meet his eyes, refused to look at Abe.

The two men shared a glance, then Abe walked away to make a phone call.

When he returned, he sat in a chair facing Abigail, eyes studying her. "I've got word your parents are at the airport getting ready to fly here. I've called and had them sent back home. Someone got to you overnight, Abi, and we have footage of a man giving your nurse an envelope. She's being interviewed right now and chances are she'll be charged as an accessory."

Abigail's eyes flew to Abe's. "They can't do that."

"They can and will, Abi. So talk to us. Tell us what that envelope said."

Luke caught the slight movement of her hand towards her sling and raised his eyes to meet Abe's. That's how it was done, he thought. "The envelope in your sling, Abi. Let's have it."

She shook her head and went to stand to walk away, but Luke's hand on her arm kept her in place. "We're trying to help here, Abi, but you're putting up roadblocks. Work with us."

"Like yesterday, when Matt got hurt, or anyone of you could have been hurt or killed?"

Abe spoke up. "It's what we do, Abi. We know the risks that are involved. So work with us. If you don't, I'm prepared to have a female officer come out and search you. Take your pick."

"You wouldn't dare!" she spit at him.

"Caleb and I are prepared to do whatever it takes to keep you safe. Your female cousin is dead, and that is likely another murder charge your uncle is facing. Jordan is dead. We're looking for Ted's son. He's likely the one in the security video. We know he got to you."

Abigail sat back, eyes on the floor, as she thought through what she had been told. "How do you stay safe, Abe, if I do say anything?"

"We can plan for a known threat, Abi. It's the unknown, like yesterday, that we can't fully plan for or avoid."

She shook her head. "I don't know, Abe. After what happened yesterday, how can I put you and your team at risk?"

Luke moved to sit beside her, wrapping her in a hug. "It's what we do, Abi. It's our business to keep people safe. If those people aren't open with us, then that's when we get into trouble. What happened yesterday may never happen again. We know who we're looking for. Caleb's team is working towards finding him. Your uncle is in custody."

"He may be in custody, but he has people out there ready to kill again." She turned tortured eyes to Luke and then to Abe, finally reaching a decision. She reached into her sling and pulled out an unmarked envelope, fingering it as she pondered her decision. Finally, she reached it towards Abe. "Please, please stay safe. I couldn't live with myself if any more of our team are even injured because of me, Abe."

Abe took the envelope, his eyes on Abigail. "Let's get one thing straight, Abi. Not one of the team blame you, least of all Matt. It's a risk we take. If they hadn't been able to find you in time, then that's what would have weighed on them for the rest of their lives."

Abigail shook her head. "I don't like it, Abe, your team putting themselves at risk."

"Abigail." Abe spoke her name and then waited until she looked up at him. He could see the devastation she had been through over the last twenty-four hours on her face and in her eyes. It would take a long time for her to recover, he knew. Who could he connect her with to talk to? Micah he had sent in with Nathaniel to talk with Greg Evans, their minister. He was really hurting from what he had heard.

"Abigail, we do what we have to. We all chose to work in this field. While we don't go out any more doing security protection, we are still trained for it. When one of our own is at risk, then we step up. And before you say anything, everyone considers you one of us. If it was a police officer, they would do the same, do everything they could to keep you safe."

She finally nodded, then laid her head back on Luke. "I'm just so tired of it all. I want my life back." She stopped speaking, lost in thought. "How long until it goes to court?"

"A few weeks at least, Abi. Maybe we'll be done with our security detail before then. Only God knows that."

She nodded, then drifted off in thought. Luke snuck a peek at her, then nodded at the envelope Abe held.

"What does it say, Abe?" His voice was quiet and monotone, trying his best not to disturb the woman he held.

Abe studied the envelope, then rose heading for his office. He returned, gloves on his hands and a clear bag open and ready for the letter. He hesitated as he looked at the letter, Luke's eyes on him.

"There's no name on it, Luke, so they could say it went to the wrong person."

Luke snorted. "We know exactly who it was meant for. What does it say?"

Abe still hesitated. "Eddie's on his way out. I called him about this. He has some more information on the security video." Abe looked up at Luke, then at Abigail. "She's been through so much, Luke, Pray we get her through this."

He pulled the letter from the envelope, then opened it, his eyes taking in the words even as his mind struggled to comprehend what was there.

"Abe?"

He heard the question in Luke's voice and finally raised his eyes, taking in Abigail's still form. "Luke, can you move her to her bedroom and then come back? I'm calling a team meeting. Everyone needs to be in on this one."

Luke stared at him for a moment, then nodded, gathering Abigail up and heading for her bedroom. Tucking a blanket around her, he stood, watching, his heart in his eyes and on his face. Lord, I love this lady. Keep her safe.

Turning, he pulled the door closed behind him and headed for the office, knowing that's where Abe would be. The team was there as was Eddie.

"Good, we're all here." Abe looked around at his team, studying the grim looks on each face. They were hurting over the events from the day before, Matt's face black and blue. "Last night, sometime during the night, someone managed to bribe a nurse to deliver an envelope to Abi. Eddie's team has identified the nurse, and she is being questioned right now. I understand she may be facing charges, Eddie?"

Eddie nodded. "She likely will. If anything, her career at the hospital is over. The hospital board is cracking down on her, given that Abigail was under police guard at the time. We have also been able to get a good clear photo of the man involved." He stopped, his eyes too studying the men around him. "He's Ted Gilmore's son, Teddy. We have people out looking for him now, but he seems to have gone to ground. Abigail is still at risk until we apprehend him. The police in her home town are with her family. No one is getting to them."

Abe waited as murmurs flew among his men, and then silence reigned again. "The letter is not pretty, guys. The depravity of these two is beyond anything I have ever seen, and we've seen a lot over the years." He stopped to compose himself, eyes on the paper he held in the bag. "Micah, I'm sorry you had to hear what you did yesterday. At this point, I'm not even sure if I should share this letter with anyone but Eddie here." He passed Eddie the letter. "Eddie can make the call, but suffice it to say, it threatens Abi in a very real, dangerous way. This man will stop at nothing but death to get back at her." Abe stopped again to compose himself. "Eddie has said that this man was responsible for his own sister's death, making it look like a home invasion. Thanks to Abi, the case was reopened, and a warrant has been issued for his arrest."

Eddie read, then read it again, his anger building and needing to be tamped down. "I would say we pass it on to my team, Abe, other than to tell your team that this is very serious and Abigail's life is at risk. He'll do anything now to get back at her, given his father's been arrested and their criminal network is being dismantled piece by piece." Eddie tucked the bag into an inside pocket of his jacket. "It's bad enough my team will have to live with this, we deal with this all the time, but there's no reason your team has to." He turned his eyes to Abe. "I would gather that Abigail has read this and refused to let you become involved."

"She has and she's trying." Abe scanned the faces of his men. "What do we do now, Eddie? I know what I would do, but I would like your input as well."

Eddie nodded, then sat back to think. Finally, he leaned forward, his voice forceful as he told Abe exactly what he would do if he was in Abe's place. Abe nodded, then voiced his thoughts, with the team weighing in. Finally, they reached a consensus of what their plans would be, and they had more than one plan.

Abe walked his uncle to his car. "Will it work, Eddie?"

Eddie shrugged. "All we can do is pray that it will. I just pray it's not too much for your team. You may need to fly out of here with her to an undisclosed location at some point. Keep an eye on Luke, though. He may help her run."

Abe laughed. "And I can bet Ian would be there helping them."

Eddie nodded. "That he would. He's offered to help each of the ladies, and I think this is the worst we've faced with them."

Abe nodded. "It is. Let me know Caleb's thoughts. He'll want to weigh in on this as well."

Luke stood behind Abe as he turned, a stern look on his face. "What did it say, Abe? How can I help her if I don't know?"

Abe heard the anguish in Luke's voice, and hesitated. "Like I said, Luke, it's not pretty. It pretty much promised her she would be dead and buried where no one would find her." Abe watched as Luke's eyes slid closed.

"That wasn't it all, was it?" Luke's voice was quiet.

"No, it wasn't, Luke. He threatened her family with the same, and he threatened you as well."

Luke stopped pacing, lost in thought. "Will our plans work, Abe? Will they keep her safe?"

"We're trying, Luke. We're trying to keep your lady as safe as we can." Abe watched as Luke began pacing again. "If needed, I'll find somewhere to fly her to that no one knows about, just like we did with Joseph and Leah."

Luke spun. "Mac would know of a place, wouldn't he?"

Abe started to laugh. "I'm sure he would. But right now, we need to focus on the next few days. Micah needs to heal from what he heard. Matt needs to heal from his beating. Your lady needs to heal, too. She goes back in what, a couple of weeks, to see about having the cast off?" At Luke's nod, Abe continued, "Then we work with what we have right now. We need to find something that keeps her occupied during the next few weeks. We have teams coming in for training over the next couple of weeks which we need to be alert and ready for."

Luke nodded as he turned to watch the rocks above the compound. "Did your father ever suspect what we'd go through and plan for it?"

Abe stopped moving, his own eyes searching the area around them. "You know, Luke, he just might." He grabbed for Luke's arm as he ran for the house. "Come on. I think you have something there."

Chapter 20

Abe tracked down Frankie late the next afternoon, as Frankie was headed into Mac's.

"Frankie, wait up."

Frankie turned, hand on the open door, and watched as Abe caught up to him. "What are you doing in town, Abe?"

Abe slid into the booth across from Frankie and nodded his thanks as the waitress poured their coffees. After she had left, he turned to Frankie. "We're setting plans in place. Luke had an idea yesterday, and we did some digging into Dad's files."

"I'm sure that was interesting." Frankie sipped his coffee, eyes on his friend.

"It was. We came up with an addition to the plan we worked out with Eddie. Can you get it to him?"

Frankie slipped the paper into his pocket. "I can, but I don't understand why you can't yourself."

"That's part of the plan, Frankie. Just talk to Eddie for me, okay?" Abe was up and gone before Frankie could reply.

Mac stood and watched, then turned to Frankie. "I'm not even going to ask what's going on."

Frankie shook his head, a smile on his face. "No, don't, because I couldn't even tell you what's going on. I'm not in the loop on this one."

Mac shook his head as he walked away, prayers lifting for his friends. He stopped, then turned and walked back to Frankie. "If you do find out, or you're talking to Abe or Luke, tell them to come find me. I have something for them."

Frankie watched in astonishment as Mac walked away. What was he up to this time, Lord? I guess this is when You'd tell me to trust, that You have a plan. All right, let's find out what it is and work it through.

Ian looked up as Abe strode into the office. "All set, Abe"

Abe nodded. "It is. Caleb got word to me that the word on the street is that there's a break in communication between us and them and that we don't trust them to keep Abi safe. I just pray this works, Ian, because if it doesn't, we won't have a second chance."

"No, we won't. The team's set up what we talking about above us. Your Dad had some good plans there."

"He did. I wish I had remembered them before."

"Don't beat yourself up, Abe." Nathaniel spoke from the doorway. "We didn't need them until now. Any word on how many?"

"Two or three is the number Caleb got to me. The preliminary hearing for her uncle is in three weeks." Abe turned to stare at the calendar on the wall, then at his team who had gathered. "I suspect the attempt will be made then, that the son will try and get to Abi and free his father at the same time."

"I think you're right, Abe." Joseph spoke up. "It makes sense that he would. Abi won't allow herself to be used as a hostage to trade for him."

"No, she won't. We just need to keep her close to the house and the safe room as much as we can."

Days passed without incident. Abigail was beginning to think the letter had been wrong, that he wouldn't try to get to her. That was until Joseph handed her a letter one day, with a legal address on it.

"Who's this from, Joseph?"

He shrugged. "It's addressed to you, but came to our office." He studied her, then it, his eyes narrowing. "You don't know that law firm, do you?"

She shook her head. "I've never heard of them. Do they even exist?"

Joseph stood for a minute, then took the letter back. "Come on, we're going out to see Abe. I have a bad feeling about this, Abi."

"I do too, Joseph. Law firms shouldn't be sending me anything here. It should go to my home address and you guys have been getting that mail for me."

Abe looked at the envelope, then at her. "Do I have your permission to open this, Abi?"

She nodded. "I really don't want to know what's in it, if I can help it."

He turned to his computer, brought up a search engine and typed in the law firm, sitting back as he studied the screen. "They don't exist, Abi." His eyes raised to hers, then he reached for a pair of latex gloves he had in his desk drawer. "I suspect this is going to be another threat, Abi. We'll have to get it to Caleb's team."

She nodded as Abe carefully slit open the envelope and withdrew the letter.

His eyes raised to her, he spoke, "I can put it back and let Caleb deal with it."

She shook her head. "That won't help, Abe. We need to know now what it says."

He nodded, then unfolded the letter. Keeping all emotion off his face was tough. "You're right, Abi. It is a threat, similar to what you had before, but this time, it's directly related to the upcoming hearing. I wish we could do your testimony by video link."

"Would the judge allow it?" Joseph asked.

"We've tried, but the defence is protesting that, saying they need her in the courtroom itself to testify." Abe sat back frustrated. "It's going to be a closed hearing but I don't like it." He looked over at Abi. "And you have no idea where these armaments are?"

She shook her head. "I don't. I haven't a clue as to what they're talking about." She rose and began to pace, her mind running through what she knew of her uncle. Then, she spun, a light in her eyes. "Can you talk to Caleb and give him an address for me?"

Abe nodded. "I can get word to him. We're supposed to be on the outs, but somehow I'll get it to him."

"Use Mac, Abe." Luke spoke from the doorway he had been standing it. "He'll gladly serve as a go-between for you."

"That he will, Luke. Okay, Abi, what's the address? Here, you can write now your arm's not in a cast.   I'll seal it into an envelope for Caleb and send one of the team in to see Mac."

"Gideon and Rebecca are headed that way for a meal. It's a perfect cover." Joseph watched as Abe thought it through, then nodded.

"That it is." He handed the envelope he had sealed everything in to Joseph. "Here. Catch him before he leaves."

Gideon found Abe in his kitchen late that night. "All delivered for you, Abe. Caleb and Eddie were actually in the cafe."

"That's good." Abe stared out into the darkness of the night, watching the clouds scudding across the sky.

"Caleb wanted to know how you all were."

Abe shrugged as he turned.   "It's wearing on the guys, Gideon.   Trying to watch Abi and train new security people at the same time. I wish I could have done it differently."

"And who would you have put off, Abe? Neither one if I know you." Gideon watched as Abe struggled with the knowledge that he couldn't have done anything differently. "How long to the hearing?"

"Middle of next week. That's when it's going to get really tough. The prosecutor thinks Abi may be on the stand for a couple of days."

"I've heard. Listen, Caleb says your guys can't be in the courtroom with her, can't even walk into the courthouse together. Sidney and I would like to take that over, escort her from here to there and stay with her. The judge and prosecutor are in agreement, the defence lawyer is against it. We've also been given permission to bring our weapons with us, given what's happened over the course of the last few weeks. Caleb will have men with us, hand picked by him and Eddie, just so nothing can be said. The defence is already saying she shouldn't be here under your guard."

Abe snorted at that. "And where would he like her? She'd be dead if she were somewhere else."

Gideon nodded. "We all know that. Eddie is sure it's a ploy by her uncle to get her somewhere he can get to her and get rid of her. It won't help his case though."

Abe sighed as he sat back down in a kitchen chair. "It's going to be tough getting her there and back. I just wonder if we'd be better sticking her somewhere in town and then moving her between days. She has to meet with the prosecutor on Monday, but that's been set at the department."

Gideon stared at his brother in law and then said, "This is taking a lot from you, Abe, or is it something else?"

"This, and that too. Just something I can't talk about, never have been able to."

"Know I'm around if you do want to talk. You know my history and what I went through."

Abe nodded as he turned his eyes back to Gideon, who had been beaten and dumped miles from Riverville when he turned 18, not able to rescue his sister from a physically abusive foster father. "Some day, maybe, Gideon. Now, about Abi. Let's see what we can come up with."

Abigail listened as Gideon pulled up to the department back door and instructed her on what she was to do. "You wait here until Sidney and I are ready to move you. In case you wonder, I used to work as an investigator for Sidney, and he's volunteered to help keep you safe today, and when you go to court. Both of us will be with you."

"I hate putting any more people at risk, Gideon."

"We don't have a choice, Abi. We can't let Abe and his team escort you in and out or even from the compound. The defence attorney is already complaining loud and long about it." His eyes searching the area, he nodded at Sidney and then Wilson who stood ready to open the door while they whisked Abigail into the building and to a small conference room that had been set aside for the attorney's use that day. Gideon knew it would be a long day for her, but a necessary one.

Abigail leaned back against the car seat late that afternoon, closing her eyes, exhausted from the day. "Where are you heading now, Gideon? I can tell it's not back to Abe's."

"No, it's not. Caleb has a place for you to stay. Doug's team and the alternate ETF team are already in place, and we have an escort there. We need to keep you away from Abe's team until you're done testifying this week. Abe's team won't take long, other than Matt and Micah, and Caleb's made arrangements for those two as well."

"I hate this, you know, don't you?" She caught his quick grin and shook her head. "If I didn't know how serious this all way, I would say you're enjoying yourself."

"It's certainly not sitting at a computer sifting through financial reports."

At his words, Abigail turned to him. "Do you know how far they got with Ted's and Jordan's financial records?"

Gideon looked over at her, then shrugged. "I haven't heard that they've found much, but that's not something I might hear. Why?"

She shook her head. "I was just wondering if anything showed up in them that would help send them away. Can you take a quick look for me, Gideon?"

"I'll see what I can to, but I'm not sure there's much to see."

"Not likely, though I did hear Jordan and his mother talking one day about offshore accounts, somewhere in the Caribbean I think."

"What brought this up for you?" Gideon searched the area around him, then pulled up to a house with an attached garage, waiting for the door to open, then pulling in. Caleb stood off to the side waiting for them.

"Just something the attorney asked today, whether I knew if they had any accounts outside the country. Somehow, I think they do."

"I'll look into it. Caleb's here, Abi, waiting for you. I'll be in in just a minute."

Caleb watched as Abigail climbed from the vehicle and walked towards him. She's exhausted, Lord, and trying so hard to trust You. Help us to help her.

"Abi, come on. I'll show you where you'll be tonight. Doug and his team are inside."

She nodded, too tired suddenly to speak. "If you would, please, Caleb. I need to lie down."

Caleb walked back through the house to the kitchen, catching up with Doug and going over their arrangements. They both turned as Gideon came in from the garage, his laptop case in his hand.

"Abigail asked if you had searched for any overseas back accounts, Caleb." Gideon watched as Caleb thought through the investigation.

"I believe we did, but I'm not aware of what we found. Frankie would likely be the one to check with, or Wilson."

"That's okay. Abi asked if I could do a search. She seems to think there are, somewhere in the Caribbean."

"Now, wouldn't that be nice to hand to the prosecutor?" Caleb shook his head. "Let me know what you find. Abi's settled likely for the night. We're good then, Doug, for the next couple of days?"

"We are, Caleb. The one team is outside, and the third team is waiting to stake out the courthouse area tomorrow night through to the end of the week. Oak City has sent in one of their teams as has Greenville."

"I just wish we could have found those armaments. That would have been a nice gift to hand to the judge."

"Caleb." Abigail's voice sounded behind him. "Did you look at Dad's old family place? It's pretty much abandoned, and no one really goes out there much. They wanted to sell it but couldn't without Ted's signature.   There are a lot of places to hide stuff."

The three men turned to watch Abigail, then Caleb had his phone out, walking away from them. When he returned, he nodded. "The chief in that area is taking a team out there now, with a sniffer dog. They'll start the search with the buildings, then work out."

"Tell them to look for a cave or something.   I can remember hearing something about a cave near a road along the back of the property. Grandpa had trouble with people staying there and trespassing."

Chapter 21

Abigail watched as a tall, grey-haired man entered the kitchen, then stood watching her.

"You must be Abigail?" At her nod, he continued, "I'm Sidney. We didn't have a chance to meet the other day. Did Gideon explain what our roles are today?"

Abigail nodded. "You're escorting me to the courthouse and back, and will be in the courtroom with me." She sighed. "Will it be over today?"

Sidney smiled. "We can pray that it is and that you're back with your fellow."

Abigail groaned. "They've got you doing that too, have they?"

Sidney laughed as he heard footsteps behind him and Gideon entered the room, a smile on his face. "That they have, Abigail. Now, you're clear on how we going about this?"

She nodded again. "Gideon has made it very clear how we're doing this. He's scary, you know."

The two men burst out into laughter at her words and the disgruntled look on her face.

"Not really, he just plays the part." Sidney turned to Gideon. "All set?"

"Just about. I'm waiting for Doug to give us the all clear before we head for the car. He should be through soon." Gideon turned to Abigail. "Just one thing, Abigail. If at any time in the courtroom, you feel uneasy or threatened, turn to the judge and let him know. He's aware that's what you've been told to do. One of the bailiffs will be standing right beside you, another behind your uncle, another to the side of the judge's bench. Sidney and I will be right behind the prosecutor's table. You go in and out through the judge's chambers, and only come in when it's your turn to testify, and then right back out."

She nodded, then looked at him, hunger in her eyes. "How's Luke? I haven't been able to talk to him in a few days."

"He's fine, Abi. He's worried about you, but sends you his love." Her mouth grew round at that and Gideon had to laugh.

"Those were his very words, Abi. I think the fellow has some strong feelings for you."

She shook her head at him as Doug entered from the garage.

"We're all set, Gideon. Are you?"

"We are, Doug. Abi's got her instructions as to how she proceeds in and out of the courthouse and into the courtroom. Everything set there?"

Doug nodded as he eyed the three standing there. "Let's move then. It's still early, but I want Abigail in before there's much traffic."

Abigail paced in the reception area to the judge's chambers, agitation evident in her movements. Gideon and Sidney watched her, two of the ETF men standing at the doorway to the courthouse corridor. So far, it had worked the way they wanted it to. Please, God, Gideon prayed, get us through today. Help us to trust that You're in control.

Luke stood and stared at the courtroom door where he knew Abigail would soon start her testimony. He was afraid for her, afraid that somehow her uncle or her cousin would get to her. He wanted to be the one with her, but understood that he couldn't. His team members mingled around him, alert to anyone and anything going on around them.

Micah stood beside him. "Did Gideon say how she's doing?"

Luke turned to Micah. "No. He didn't. I didn't think he would." He looked around, eyes watchful for something off. He could feel it, just couldn't see it. "How are you doing, Micah? Abe has never let you say what you heard."

Micah shook his head. "No, you don't need to know what she said or what her uncle said to her. I'm just glad that he's behind bars. He needs to go away for a long time."

Luke nodded. "I get that, Micah. I just wish it had been different."

"It wasn't, Luke, so we move on from that. That's where our trust in God comes in, that He leads and allows what happens in our lives."

Luke nodded, then settled back again a wall. It was going to be a long day, he thought, as he watched ETF officers and patrol officers walking the corridors around him. What kind of man was this after all, he wondered?

Abigail turned as a bailiff approached her and spoke, "Miss Gilmore, we're ready for you now. If you follow me, your escorts will be around you as well. When we get in the courtroom, I'll take you right to the stand.

I'll be beside you all the time. As your friends have indicated to you, don't be afraid to turn to the judge if you feel anything off. If you need to stop testifying, just say so." He waited for her nod, then lead the way into the courtroom.

Abigail kept her eyes straight ahead, shivering slightly as she felt her uncle's eyes upon her. How did a family have such a diversity in people, one good, two siblings so evil their children were evil?

Sworn in, she sat, her eyes fixed on the prosecutor. She could sense movement at the defendant's table, but she refused to look that way, not wanting to see the man who had caused so much trauma in her life and those of her friends and so many countless others.

Following the questions asked of her, she gave her testimony, her voice wavering with emotion when she got to the part with Matt. Her uncle's attorney was on his feet, objecting, but quickly sitting back down when the judge ordered him to and told him that it was part of the testimony and it wouldn't be taken from the record.

Abigail breathed a sigh of relief as she finished the first of her testimony, then waited for the judge to let the defending attorney begin. Her hands tightened on each other. Then she forced herself to relax. She was not giving him that much control over her.

She was not prepared for her uncle's attorney to start bringing in charge after charge that she had faced. The judge took one look at her, then called the two attorneys to the bench. She could hear the low voices, then waited as the attorneys went back to their respective tables.

"Miss Gilmore, you understand what these charges are, don't you?" The oily voice of the attorney grated against her.

"No, I'm sorry. I don't."

"What do you mean? These charges are all against you."

"Where were they filed?"

"I'm asking the questions here, not you. Now answer mine."

"I will if you tell me where the charges were filed."

He glared at her and began reading off towns, looking up at her silence.

She sat, shaking her head. "I have never ever been in those towns. The dates and times they're giving, I was here in the courthouse, transcribing trials."

"That just can't be." His voice rose. "We have official records."

"Then I suggest you look further. I have no idea what those charges are, but I can tell you they're not against me."

"Move on, please. She's answered your question twice. Next question." The judge was losing patience with the attorney, Abigail could hear it in his voice.

Question after question shot her way, and she was beginning to get tired of answering the same question asked in a different manner. Finally, she had had enough.

"I'm sorry. I refuse to answer any more questions from you, unless they are brand new. I have answered every question you have asked, even five or six times because it was couched in different phrasing."

The defence attorney spluttered but before he could speak, the judge spoke up.

"You've tried my patience today, sir, and the patience of a competent witness. Now, if you have no further questions for the witness, we'll be adjourning for the day and Miss Gilmore will be excused from further testimony."

"No further questions, Your Honour."

As Abigail turned to step down, a sudden movement at the defendant's table drew everyone's attention to her uncle. He was rising, hand shackled in front of him, but with a gun in his hand, pointed directly at her. As shots rang out, the bailiff had her down and to safety. Gideon and Sidney had their weapons out, but the bailiff standing by the judge reacted first, his weapon out and firing. A surprised look came over Ted Gilmore's face, then he sank back, the weapon falling from his hand.

Gideon and Sidney holstered their weapons as they moved towards Abigail. Their first concern was getting her out of the courtroom. The bailiff with her moved them quickly back to the judge's chamber, the judge on their heels, closing the door behind them and locking it. The judge took one look at Abigail, then reached for water.

"Here, drink this." He smiled as she tried to say thank you. "No, no worries. We'll get this sorted out. Here, come into my chambers. You'll be more comfortable there." A quick glance up at Gideon and Sidney and he knew they understood what he was maneuvering her to do.

Abe's team spun as they heard the shots from the courtroom, ready to go into action, but constrained by the fact that they weren't law officers. They watched as the ETF team and other officers spread out, some heading for the judge's chambers, some for the courtroom door.

Abe's hand was on Luke's shoulder. "We'll get word as soon as we can, Luke. Just stand tight." Abe reached for his phone as it chimed. "It's Gideon, Luke. Abi's okay and out of there."

Luke relaxed at that. "As long as she's safe, that's the main thing." His eyes traveled among the crowd mingling there, stopping on one man. "Abe, that man there. It could be Jordan's twin."

"Where?" Abe's eyes followed to where Luke had indicated. He looked around, but couldn't see an officer he recognized. "Come on, Luke, Joseph. Let's go have a talk with that man."

They followed him as he walked carefully and slowly from the corridor, not as one would expect a person to be walking given the excitement. Once outside, they quickened their steps and drew up to him, causing him to stop. Frankie was on his way into the courthouse and stopped as he watched, then approached the men.

"Frankie, just the person we wanted to see. We were just explaining to this gentleman that we wanted to talk with him. I would have said he was Jordan Gilmore, except I know he's dead." Abe stood in front of the man, refusing to let him walk away.

"Let's see some identification, please." Frankie held out his hand, then at a move from the man, had him down and handcuffed. He searched him, drawing out a wallet and then a handgun. "My goodness, sir, a handgun in the courthouse? That's gets you a ride downtown at the very least. Let's see who you are." He opened the wallet and began pulling out identification, the picture matching the man, but names different. He finally stopped at one. "I think this one is the correct one. Teddy Gilmore, you're under arrest."

Frankie handed him off to a patrol officer to take to the department, then turned to Abe. "What's going on, Abe? We have word of shots fired in the courtroom, then find you confronting this man?"

Abe shrugged. "I don't know, Frankie. We heard the commotion in the courtroom, then saw this man walking away. Luke thought he looked enough like Jordan Gilmore to be a family member, so we went with his hunch."

"Your hunch was right, Luke. Come on back inside. I need to get to the courtroom and see what's up. I know they have Abigail locked up in the Judge's chambers, so no one can get to her." Frankie stopped in his walk along the corridor, turning to stare behind him. "If that's his son, then he's the last one we've been looking for. In that case, it may all be over, Luke, and you can see your lady."

Luke nodded, not bothering to deny that Abigail was his lady. It was just too much effort today, he thought.

Abigail spun around as she heard her name. Frankie stood in the doorway, his eyes on her, compassion on his face.

"Frankie, what's going on? No one will tell me."

"Come, sit for a minute, Abigail. I need to let you know what's going on, but I want you to sit and relax. Luke's fine, in cause you're wondering, as are all of Abe's team." He could see the visible way she relaxed as his words. "Now, as to what happened. Your uncle bribed a cleaner to bring in the weapon and tape it under the table this morning so that it was put in after the courtroom was swept. I understand that's changing. Your uncle is dead. He can no longer threaten you or your family."

Abigail's eyes slid closed. "He's dead? What about his son?"

"He was caught today. Your Luke spotted him and I found Abe, Joseph and your Luke outside stopping him from walking away. He had a wallet full of fake identification that he can't explain away. He'll not trouble you either." He watched her face, trying to read her thoughts.

"It's over? It's really over?" She could barely speak the words.

"It is pretty much, Abigail. We have some work to do, but you can go home any time you want. But first, I have someone out in the reception area who would really like to see you."

Abigail shook her head. "Please, Frankie, not right now. Tell him I need some time. I really need some time to process everything."

Frankie watched, not sure she was making the right decision, but finally nodded. "He'll be hurt and disappointed, Abigail. Just don't wait too long to see him, okay?"

She finally nodded and then turned away as Frankie studied her face.

Luke stood, eyes glued to the door behind where Abigail was, waiting for her to come out. Frankie stepped through the door, closing it behind him. He hesitated, then approached Luke.

"I'm sorry, Luke. She asked for some time to process what's gone down. She needs some space and time. I've told her not to take too long."

Luke's face fell in disappointment, but he nodded. "She's been through a lot and need to work it all out. She'll be tired of seeing you people by the time the next couple of days are over." He turned to search for Abe. "I wonder, if when she's through, if she'd like Ian to fly her out to her folks."

"Are you sure about that, Luke? She may not come back." Frankie wasn't sure Luke was doing the right thing.

"I am, but I don't see Ian anywhere." He turned once again to search for Abe, but found him at his shoulder.

"I've sent Ian to get her people, Luke. She's going to need her Mom."

Luke nodded. "She will. I have to step back for now, Abe, and it hurts." Luke walked out of the room and away from his friends.

Frankie watched, slowly pocketing his pen. "He's hurting, Abe, and the only one who can help him here on earth has refused to see him.”

“He’ll get there, Frankie. His trust in God is strong as is hers. They’re meant to be.”

Chapter 22

Abigail signed the final piece of paper, stacked them tidily and slid them across the table to Frankie. "That's it, I think, Frankie. That should do it."

"I think it does, Abigail. Now, what are you going to do?"

"I can't go back to work in the court reporter's office, knowing that my uncle had those people killed and injured. I know I'm not responsible for that, but I can't face working there any more. I'm not sure where I'll end up. I don't want to go back home."

"I think this town has grown on you." Frankie pulled a business card from his shirt pocket. "Here, talk to this lady. She could use some of your transcription skills."

Curious, Abigail took the proffered card and read it. "Are you serious? This lady does big time legal cases."

Frankie nodded with a smile. "She's heard about you and how wonderful your work is. She's in search of a transcriptionist and thinks you'll work out fine. She wants you to start on Monday morning at 9."

"What a minute, Frankie. I haven't even met her."

"No, you haven't, but she's a sister of the judge you testified under in your uncle's case. He put in a good word for you, and that was enough for her. It's up to you to make good now."

"That I will do my best. Thank you. I see your hand in this." She stood, hesitant to walk freely once more.

"It feels strange, doesn't it, Abigail?" When she looked at him, he smiled. "You can walk about without worrying, without looking over your shoulder. I suggest a nice walk along the river. I heard the wind's pleasant at this time of day."

"What are you up to?" Abigail eyed him suspiciously.

"Nothing, Abigail. I just think you could use some fresh air." A sparkle of mischief shone in his eye.

Abigail stood on the river bank, listening to the musical tinkle of the water over the rocks on the edge, the birds and insects, the faint rustle of the leaves, and breathed in the scents and smells. Frankie was right, she thought. I needed this. The last few weeks have been so full and violent and hectic I've taken my eyes off what is important. Thank You, dear Lord, for the reminder of what matters most.

She turned and stopped, staring at the man standing a few feet behind her, just watching her. He reached for her and she took his hand.

"Luke, where did you come from?"

"A little bird told me I might find you here. It seems he was right."

Abigail laughed. "I wonder if it was the same bird who told me I needed some fresh air." She stopped, her eyes taking in his face. "How are you, Luke?"

"Much better now." His head tilted as he watched her, then he laughed as his comment made sense to her. "I've missed you, sweetheart."

"I missed you too. Let's not do this again, okay?"

"That's fine with me. Now, if you're interested, I might be talked into buying you some dinner and catching up on what's gone on."

"I would like that. Thank you, Luke."

Two hours later, Abigail sat back in her seat at the restaurant. "Did we really go through all that, Luke?"

He nodded. "We did. Thankfully, we came through relatively unscathed, considering what went on. Micah's dealt with what he heard, and he still hasn't told me what you said." He held up a hand as she opened her mouth. "Sweetheart, I don't need to know what was said. I know it was bad. Matt's made a full recovery, and Sarah doted on him, which he enjoyed by the way."

"And now us?"

"And now us. Abi, you were my best friend growing up. I'm sorry we parted ways. I'm sorry you had to go through what you did. But I'm not sorry you're back in my life."

She stared at him, then laughed. "Why do I feel like there's a but coming?" He laughed with her. "We have been through so much, Luke, more than what you'll ever know I went through. I'm still trying to deal with the fact that it was family and that an uncle was ready to resort to murder more than once. Dad's having issues dealing with this. He's hurting."

"I'm sure he is. I guess this is where our trust in God comes in, knowing that He's in charge but allows things like this to happen. Murphy's always telling us God has a plan and a purpose. Sometimes, I wish He'd let us in on those plans."

Abigail laughed again. "You and me both."

Luke stood, dropped money on the table for their meal, and pulled Abigail to her feet. "If you're not too tired, let's walk for a while and make some plans. Now that you're back in my life, I have no intention of letting you go."

Abigail smiled and nestled her hand closer into Luke's. This was what she had dreamed of as a teenager, with a teenage crush on the handsome boy next door. Lord, I have no idea where this is going, but You do. Thank you for Your leading.

Abigail was laughing hard enough at the teasing going on in Abe's kitchen that she could hardly finish the meal she had prepared.

"Murphy and Ian, you two need to stop, now, or I'll never finish the meal I promised to make for you."

Ian grinned, unrepentant. "That's okay. Then you'd just have to come back and make another meal for us."

She shook her finger at him as she tucked the potatoes and carrots around the roast. "There, now go put it on the table, and find your ladies. Your meal is already."

Ian took the platter she shoved at him and walked away, shaking his head. Murphy stood watching, an amused look on his face. "I notice that we're short two table settings."

"You did, did you?"

He nodded. "I gather that you and Luke aren't joining us."

"Not tonight, Murphy. We have other plans." Luke spoke from behind Murphy.

Murphy shook his head as he watched the two walk away, then turned as he heard someone beside him. Abe stood there.

"Not eating with us, I guess, Murphy?"

"They tell me no. But I am. That meal smells delicious."

Luke tucked Abigail into his truck, then walked around to climb into the driver's seat, fingering the small box in his jacket pocket as he did so. Abigail watched as he drove away, heading for a spot that had become special to them, a spot near the river with a picnic table and bench.

Their own meal over and the remnants packed away, Luke reached for Abigail's hand and they just sat, watching the sun's rays as it faded towards the horizon.

"Abigail, when I thought I had lost you, I didn't know how I would go on." Luke turned to watch her. "I can't lose you. Will you be mine, walk with me through the life that God gives us, be the cherished part of my heart that completes me?"

Abigail felt the tears start and blinked rapidly to clear her eyes, even as she nodded. "I will," she responded, her voice barely above a whisper, lifting her face for his kiss, then watching as he pulled a beautiful ring with an emerald stone from its box and placing it on her finger.

"God brought to this point, sweetheart. I am thankful each day for the way He has."

Abigail nodded. "If we hadn't been through what we had, we wouldn't be able to trust Him in the way we need to. My prayer, dear one, is that our trust in Him grows with each day."

"Amen to that." Luke gathered her close in his arms as the setting sun shone in its glory, just for them they thought.

Dear Readers:

Thank you for choosing the story of Luke and his Abigail. They were through a lot, but their trust in God shone through. That's what trust in God is, the utmost confidence that He knows best for us, that we follow as He leads, our hands in His.

Proverbs 3:5 and 6 were my Mom's life verses. Every book, every card she ever gave to family contains those verses. I miss my Mom so much some days. I just want to talk to her once more, but can't as God called her home very suddenly in 2010. Tears come when I read or hear those verses but I cherish the memory of how much Mom trusted God and showed it in her daily walk.

Where are you with your trust in God? Still working on it? It's a lifetime task, to trust.

God bless each one of you.

Ronna

www.ingramcontent.com/pod-product-compliance
Lightning Source LLC
Chambersburg PA
CBHW070457200726
48293CB00007B/2260